STOLEN QUEEN

A DARK CAPTIVE ROMANCE

JESI DONOVAN

To all the ladies that have been held back by someone or something: may you find the strength to take your power back.

CONTENTS

ARCTURUS

Bray is afraid of nothing. He sinks his teeth into the officer's throat and pulls back as the man screams; the echo of his yells lasts longer than his life.

Blood drips down Bray's face coating his muzzle and chest in slick red liquid. One look in my direction tells me that he's finished. He drops the leftover skin and sinew onto the ground and leads the way.

We slink through the streets of the Cersei district under the cover of darkness. The moon shines high above, casting a silhouette onto cobblestones when we emerge from the shadows. Curtains are drawn and doors are locked tight when people see us prowling the street.

The Cersei district is used to wolf shifters. The men and women in charge are all shifters of some sort. But they know just by glancing our way that we do not belong, that we are meant to be feared. Or perhaps they recognize our faces from the newspaper. The Mad Kings, they call us, a filthy moniker devised by men that can't destroy us. Whatever it is, it convinces them to stay behind closed doors and let us raid their district in peace.

Fausto, Bray, and I live in the Forbidden Lands. We have not been tempered by the magic of Meira'mor. Our coats are not shiny from brushing and our size is not muted to appease the magical folk. In the Forbidden Lands, anything goes.

Bray is the first to approach the mansion. The hair on his back bristles in anger as he turns to look at me for approval. His bright yellow eyes look putrid in the midnight light. Our pack is connected and I can hear his thoughts even though his muzzle never opens. *She's here. I can feel it.*

Fausto nods his head in agreement. Elspeth's blood calls to us like a siren, demanding that we give her our full attention. There isn't a light on in the house, but I can smell her from all the way out here. *East wing,* I tell them with my eyes braced on a lonely window, *third floor.*

They take off. I hear their scattered thoughts in my head. Bray is saying *kill kill kill* over and over again while Fausto is trying to determine the best way to get to her room without running into trouble. I urge them on silently as I stand guard and watch for lights to come on or passersby to stop and question my presence. But it never happens.

Fausto disappears around the west side of the building while Bray scales the tree outside Elspeth's window. I hear them snarling as they work together to find a way in without attracting attention. Fausto finds an open cellar door while Bray decides that breaking Elspeth's bedroom window will cause more harm than good. I commend them equally.

The Avermo household remains still as Bray and Fausto search through the darkness for Elspeth's room. Their presence grows closer with each passing minute. They're almost in the home stretch when the screams begin.

I want to be inside so bad. I want to smell the fear radiating off Cason when he realizes what's happening. I want to drink in Amaris' anger when her husband explains in shame why Elspeth was stolen in the dead of night. I want to watch their marriage crumble and their silly little district fall into ruin when they lose their heir.

I can only watch from afar as my pack ravages its way through the house. Lights come on and shrieks are quick to follow.

The Mad Kings have arrived.

ELSPETH

I've been prepared for this moment my entire life. When the screams jolt me from my sleep, my body breaks into a cold sweat as I leap from my bed and head for the closet. My father's words come back to me in waves.

Take the tunnels.

Make sure to close the door so no one sees you.

Go to the police.

He's been giving me these instructions for as long as I can remember. My father drilled them into my head from the day I turned five. He never let me move rooms because he was afraid that I wouldn't remember where to go.

The hidden passage in my closet is the first place that I head for. I barely graze the handle of the closet door when I'm grabbed from around the waist and yanked backward. A wolf with blood all over its face has me in its clutches.

"No!" I scream as I beat the beast on the muzzle and shoulders, anything to escape his grasp. I have never seen this wolf before. "Let me go! I'm not the one you're looking for!" My heart races as he takes me toward the window. I catch a glimpse of his eyes in the moonlight and I'm met with dark, red pupils. I'm mesmerized for a moment, struck dumb by the anger and malevolence I see looking back at me.

With the window open, he stands on the sill, giant paws eclipsing half the opening. With his teeth buried in my nightgown, I have two choices: let him pull me to the ground and possibly get injured, or hold on. I choose the latter. Sometimes you have to pick survival.

I wrap my arms around his wide neck and it seems impossible that his existence is real. My father is a wolf shifter and he's not nearly this large. My mother is even smaller than that. But holding onto this monstrous beast opens my eyes to a new sort of creature.

He slams into the ground and I grunt with pain from the jarring stop. Ahead of him is another wolf that's even larger. They exchange communication tele-pathically, a skill that only connected packs have. I extract myself from the wolf's fur and try to flee but it's hopeless. With his teeth still enclosing my night-gown, I only make it a foot before the seams rip and

I'm left standing there in a tattered piece of silk and my panties.

My jaw drops open as I try to grab what's left of my sleeping clothes. A chunk has been taken out of the bottom and half the right side is flayed open, but I pinch the remaining fabric together in hopes of preserving my dignity. Where is my father? He should be coming to save me soon.

A third wolf appears out of nowhere. He wears the blood of my household like a second skin. His yellow eyes look me up and down with lascivious delight and I back away from him instantly. But it's the largest of the three that grabs me by the wrist and throws me over his shoulder.

The home that I've known since I was a child gets smaller in the distance as he carries me off. I scramble to escape, but every movement causes what's left of my nightgown to shift or tear, not to mention the wolf's grip is ironclad. Even if I had no shame, I wouldn't be able to escape.

We reach the outskirts of town with the other two wolves following closely behind. I catch myself looking from one to the other as I scream for help, but no one opens their door. The red-eyed wolf looks like he's laughing at me. The yellow-eyed one looks like he's daring someone to open the door so he can rip them limb from limb. For the first time in my life, it occurs to me that the residents of the Cersei district are cowards. I could scream bloody murder all night and no one would come out to help me.

There's a car at the edge of the district and a single man stands outside beneath a light. He has a cigarette between his lips; I see the orange glow when I'm tossed to the ground in front of him. The driver grabs me with ease and shoves me into the car as I watch the three wolves shift back into their human forms. They are smaller, but barely.

My heart nearly stops when I recognize the largest of the three. *I know them,* I think to myself. Or at least I know *of* them. I've seen their pictures splashed across the front page of the newspaper. I've heard stories about what they're capable of. They're the Mad Kings. My stomach turns and I wretch the contents of my dinner onto the floor of the car.

"I'm not cleaning that up," says one of the men.

The driver peeks inside and gives me a look before releasing a frustrated sigh. "I should have brought the witch," he mumbles to himself.

"No," another man says with a glare, "the fewer people involved, the better. Take care of it when we get back. There is no time."

All four of the men climb inside the vehicle. The driver gets behind the wheel as the largest man gets into the passenger seat. The other two slip into the back with me. One's nose scrunches in disgust as he steps over my vomit. He still has blood all over his front and there are deep wounds in his arms that leak as the car drives us away from the scene of my kidnapping. If he were still in his shifted form, he could heal himself. But instead, he sits there and pokes at his scrapes as he relives the night with his friends.

Bits and pieces of the conversation make sense. Their arrival on the third floor tripped a sensor. Two guards stationed in rooms near mine were the first to emerge from their beds. My father took an extra few moments to arrive, but he was already shifted when he made it up the stairs.

Other details make me question what happened.

One of the guards let them through the line. My father knew that they had come for me. The third wolf was a lookout.

I've accepted for years that I'm not the smartest nor the most talented witch in Meira'mor, but I thought I could put two-and-two together. Listening to the three of them discuss the evening's events make me second-guess myself.

Why did they come tonight? Why were there only two guards on duty? Who let them pass? Why did my father know to arrive shifted?

My head spins as the car barrels down the road. Dirt kicks up all around us. I can't make out the Cersei district anymore; it's just a blip in the rearview mirror.

If I remember correctly, their names are Arcturus, Fausto, and Bray. They're the Mad Kings, known for their heathen rule over the Forbidden Lands. My father said they might come for me one day, but he never told me why. As they laugh together, my stomach churns once more.

What do they want from me? And what are they going to do to get it?

BRAY

At twelve years old, Arcturus knew that he would be the first point of the Forbidden Lands crown when he turned eighteen. With Fausto and I in his pack, there was no way that he could lose. He just had to bide his time until he became of age and challenged the current leading pack. He took us from nobodies and made us the most important men in the land.

In whispers, we shared our hopes and dreams for the future. Arcturus wanted to bring honor back to our race. He wanted people to fear wolf shifters once more. "We are not second-class citizens to the dragons," he would say, "we are stronger and more capable." He saw our rule as a chance to strike fear into the hearts of the men and women in the mainlands. No longer would we cower in the shadows or work side-by-side with the witches and demons cast out in disgrace. We would solidify our place in history as the most fearsome creatures to live on this side of the portal.

Fausto was a revolutionary that wanted to see the Forbidden Lands go through its own Industrial Revolution. He wanted better homes for the packs and more opportunities. He saw life in the Forbidden Lands as less of a toxic wasteland and more of a blessing in disguise. "We don't have to be hampered by the rules of Meira'mor," he'd announce as he shook with excitement, "we could create something they'd be envious of."

I just wanted our former glory back. We'd shrunken over the last few decades due to extreme loss. The Officials in Meira'mor were always seeking to tame us outsiders. Every year it felt like a few more packs disappeared, returning to the mainlands to stick it out with the norms. They preferred life in suburbia with a handbook of rules over the lawless existence we'd created as an outcast district. "We could change the future of the Forbidden Lands if we regained our power," I tried to tell them. But Arcturus and Fausto weren't too sure about my crazy dreams. They said that I didn't know what I was talking about, but they were wrong. I was the only one who was thinking long-term.

Somewhere along the way, we were dubbed the Mad Kings. Maybe it was because Arcturus killed the former leaders singlehandedly. Instead of sparing their lives and allowing them to live in shame among us, he tore them limb from limb and left them in the town square to rot for a week before he allowed their bodies to be claimed by their families.

Maybe it was because Fausto's plan for a better community only included his dream. While others offered their suggestions, Fausto built up the Forbidden Lands how *he* wanted them to look. It caused controversy among the packs, presumably being the thing that led to another half dozen leaving in anger. While many could appreciate his vision for the future, many were put off by the way he achieved it.

But I was the one with the foolproof plan. I was the one that suggested stealing back what was ours. "Our forefathers were robbed of their future by men and women that belonged to the mainlands. We deserve to take what's ours. We deserve a Queen of the blood." We could have taken anyone as our Queen, but I wanted what should have been promised to us if wasn't for a brave little mainlander sixty years before.

I spoke the words that no one else wanted to speak. I said what everyone else was too afraid to say. The Forbidden Lands had lost their Queen an eternity ago, long before the three of us had taken power. If we wanted to keep it, we'd have to do something drastic.

"No one could deny our rule if we mated the last

remaining heir of Alize Nikae. We could cement our place in history." It was a farfetched plan if you thought about it hard enough. What was the smallest leading wolf pack in the history of the Forbidden Lands going to do that previous packs hadn't? How could we achieve what they could not?

If that wasn't bad enough, we had to trace Alize's lineage from the day of her kidnapping. It meant asking questions, doing research, and raising the curious gaze of men and women all through the lands. After all these years, they were confused as to why we'd bring up the name and history of their forgotten ruler.

But every man has a purpose in history. Even the lowly person that shoveled the streets after a hard winter's snow had a purpose. And I grew up believing that mine was to bring the Forbidden Lands back to what they once were. Arcturus dreamt of leadership; I dreamt of a legacy.

I did the legwork. I found out where the men had taken Alize all those decades ago. I followed the trail until it dead-ended at Elspeth Avermo. I put people in her home to keep a protective eye on her. I readied myself for a battle.

They say the tides change with the moon. I waited until I had all my ducks in a row before I presented my case to Arcturus and Fausto. At first, they laughed at me, but I know what happened when they went to bed that night.

Fausto paced across his room and questioned the legacy he was leaving behind. It was nice being the man who'd brought better living conditions and food to the Forbidden Lands, but how many had he driven away to make it happen? Could he redeem his reputation if he helped restore the blood of the old Queen?

Arcturus tossed and turned in his bed as he contemplated what the history books would write about him. The largest wolf in over a century and all he'd accomplished was a rein of terror. The packs were afraid and no one could trust him to lead in earnest. Would they change their minds if he had a Queen by his side?

When morning rolled around, they said yes to my plan. They each had a reason to want Elspeth Avermo, but we all needed her as a salve for our pride. Her presence would reinvigorate the packs. She would reunite the Forbidden Lands as they once were. And when we'd filled her belly with a dozen wolf pups, everyone would know that our rule was the strongest.

Desire ruled over *us* like the moon. And soon our desire to prove ourselves would be quenched by the tight little body of the woman that was always meant to be the Queen of these lands.

ELSPETH

They don't bother to cuff me or tie me up; they're not afraid I'll be able to run away. I try to pretend that I'm offended by their assessment, but two-story tall gates topped with spikes encircle the property. Even if I could run away, there is nowhere for me to go.

"You don't have to do this," I quietly protest as the driver helps me out of the car and escorts me behind the three men. "I'm not the person they're looking for. I'm a witch. I'm a—"

"*What?*" The largest of the three men stops and turns on his heel so quickly that we run into him. His body is like steel when I face plant into his chest. He is all muscles and washboard abs; the kind of man you'd see on the cover of a magazine. "You're not a *witch*, Elspeth." He says the word with disdain, making goosebumps crop up on my biceps. "Who told you that?"

My mouth opens and closes repeatedly as I try to form words. The grip on my arm tightens and I look up at the driver to see him nod his head once. He wants me to talk, but I don't know how to explain myself when the answer seems so self-explanatory. "I-I just know I am. I'm a healer. Or, well, I-I heal others. I can make elixirs and tinctures. It's the only skill I have."

"Bray," the tallest turns to the man whose gaze scares me to the core, "is this the right girl?"

If he wasn't covered in blood, Bray would be a good-looking man. He has a square jawline and soulful brown eyes that make you want to melt, a far cry from the yellow I saw when he was shifted. He's tall and broad-shouldered but in an unassuming sort of way. "You are Elspeth Avermo," Bray accuses as he steps forward. He leaves no room for debate.

I stupidly nod my head yes in agreement. Perhaps if I said no, they'd take me back to the Cersei district and leave me alone. Or just let me go outside the gates and I could find my way back on foot. Or maybe I'm just a wishful thinker.

"This is the right girl, Arc," Bray tosses a look at the larger one. "She's been brainwashed."

"Hey, wait a minute," I start to speak up with a frown deepening on my forehead. "I'm not brainwashed. I *am* a witch. I'm not even a very powerful one," I go on. "My father said I wasn't even powerful enough to see The Council when I come of age. He said they might force me to leave Meira'mor if they knew how weak I was." My father told me that non-magical people can't live on this side of the portal; it's why he hid me from anyone in power.

The unnamed man throws his head back laughing. His long hair goes with it and a waterfall of blonde drips down his back. "I swear if we risked it all for the wrong woman, Bray." His words sound like they're going to end with a threat.

But now I remember their names from the news articles. Hearing Bray's name a second time triggers a core memory. Five years ago they raided our town and took all of our winter stores, leaving us with nothing when the snow came. My father led the team that went out hunting every day for food, not just for our table, but for the tables of everyone in Cersei. "You're a monster," I turn to the blood-covered Bray Sladec. "You nearly killed my brother that winter."

"What?" Bray glares. "What winter?"

I forget that they can't read my mind. I was continuing the train of thought I had about the year they wreaked havoc on Cersei. "Five years ago. I know it was the three of you," I look accusingly at the other two. Their names come back to me like a forgotten memory. The largest of the men is Arcturus Holbrook, the fierce leader of the Forbidden Lands. He killed a dozen of our men that year. The blonde is Fausto Drayton, known for his cunning mind and keen ability to find a way out of any situation. "I knew who you were when you shifted back at the car. I should have screamed louder." I try to take a step back, but the driver's hand on my arm stops me, holding me in place.

Fausto is still laughing, but the edge of his chuckle is wrought with evil. "Funny, because people were locking their doors when they saw us. They must remember *that winter*," he mocks. "Nobody was going to save you, princess. They would rather watch you get torn apart before challenging the three of us."

"You're wrong," I glare up at him. "My father would have saved me. What did you do to him?" I try to yank my arm out of the driver's grasp again, but he doesn't even break a sweat as he digs his fingers into my tender skin.

"Miss," he looks down at me, "don't make me have to chase you down." There is a threatening edge to his tone that makes me stop squirming. I don't know who he is, but he seems like the type to kill first and ask questions later.

Arcturus is the one to respond. He steps forward to line up with Bray, making me feel claustrophobic as I'm surrounded by shifters. "Your father will be lucky to survive the night. After what his family did to us, he deserves to die a slow and painful death."

Red colors my cheeks in anger. "He didn't do anything to you!" I snarl at Arcturus as if I'm capable of hurting him the way he's hurt me.

"Wrong," he roars back in my face. "He kept your powers hidden from you. He kept you hidden from the world. He kept you hidden from *us*." Arcturus' teeth are bared as if he wants to reach forward and take a chunk out of me. "He might not have been the one to steal the Queen all those years ago, but he kept *our* Queen hidden."

My head is spinning. I am nobody's Queen. I have no powers, not really. My father couldn't have hidden them from me because they don't exist. He couldn't have hidden me because he allowed me the freedom to leave the house whenever I wanted. Sure, I had to have a bodyguard, but that was for my own protection. He said that the Kings of the Forbidden Land were forever trying to steal little girls like me. He convinced me that every home in Cersei was equipped with hidden doors and secret entrances so that way the daughters could escape during a raid.

"You're a liar." My breath comes in ragged strips. "My father didn't do anything of that. He's a good man. He's only protected me from men like you." I can't meet their eyes anymore. I stare at the ground and take in the scorched earth beneath me. The terrain looks as though it's been devoid of grass for a century.

I bury my heart in the grains of soil as fear wraps me around my shoulders like a blanket.

"Take her to the dungeon, Roth," Arcturus shakes his head at the driver.

Fausto huffs in disagreement, "Arc."

The driver pulls me toward the looming castle, but not before I hear, "We don't have a choice. We can't do anything with her in this state. She needs to be broken."

Roth pulls me along as if I weigh nothing. "Let me give you a piece of advice," he whispers as we walk through the doors of the castle, "give them what they want. The dungeons are not the place for a nice girl like yourself."

I resolve to kick and scream every step of the way. I don't want his advice or kindness. I'm not giving in to those shifters upstairs. They can do whatever they want to me, but I will not give them what they want.

I will not break.

FAUSTO

"We need to test her blood." I have a growing headache, a combination of frustration and anger that feels like it's drilling holes into my skull. If the girl we just kidnapped *isn't* Alize Nikae's granddaughter, we've made a grave error. Not only that, we've revealed our hand to the mainlanders. They'll know that we're coming for her. "Yes, we need to test her blood," I mumble again.

Arcturus scoffs and heads for the castle, his feet kicking up dirt in his wake. "We could *smell* her blood, Fausto. It's her," he declares. "There's no reason for us to believe any differently."

Should I humor him and let it go? Mention that she called herself a witch? "Something isn't right about this, is all." I follow behind him and Bray with an uneasy feeling in the pit of my stomach. "Did you hear what she said about not being powerful?" We need a powerful Queen by our sides. The packs of the Forbidden Lands will never believe us if we present them with a weak little thing that believes she's a healer.

Bray directs us to the kitchen; he's always hungry and after a raid, he's starving. "*I heard* that she trusts her father implicitly. I especially heard that he didn't want her going to The Council. They would have told her she was a shifter and started asking questions about her abilities. He wanted to keep her locked up forever, so he lied to her." He says it like he's got it all figured out.

I don't mention that we just sent her with Roth to be locked in the dungeons until we see fit; the irony would be too much for Bray. We saved her from being locked up only to lock her up in a different location. "I'm just saying, I think we need to test her blood to make sure. Even if she is Alize's daughter, she should have some kind of magic in her veins. And not the kind that makes potions or whatever she called them."

Arcturus grabs a gallon of milk and pours himself a cup. As he reaches into the spice cabinet to pull out the cinnamon, his other hand is reaching into the silverware drawer to grab a spoon. "We're not vampires, Fausto," he says patiently.

"I'm not saying I want to drink her blood," I

respond with a glare as he deliberately misunderstands me. "I just think a simple slit of her wrist and a lick or two will do the job. We'll know for sure that it's her. Then we can decide from there if she's what we are looking for."

In the middle of making a double-decker sandwich, Bray stops spreading mayonnaise on his third slice of bread to give me an angry look. "What do you mean, *decide if she's what we are looking for*? She's Alize's granddaughter. She's exactly what we're looking for. She's why we made this whole fucking suicide run."

I'm not traditionally the voice of reason among the pack. Arcturus tends to be in charge of that territory with his level-headed thinking in the face of chaos—unless his pride is at stake, in which case he turns into a monster. But I feel like the only one who understands what might happen if we present a witch to the packs of the Forbidden Lands. Either more of our men and women will leave, or someone will challenge Arcturus. Even if their death is certain, the wolves in this part of Meira'mor would rather risk dying than life with a witch in charge.

"Be fucking real right now, Bray," I pin him with the same look that he gave me, "we cannot present her to the packs if she isn't a shifter. They'll eat her alive. Better yet, they'll eat all of us alive. Including you," I tilt my chin at Arcturus. "None of us are immune to our brethren turning their backs on us."

Bray slams the mayonnaise down on the kitchen counter and starts walking toward me. "Are you threatening our rule?" He hisses. "Because we don't fucking need you, Fausto. I'll take you out right now. There doesn't have to be three points on this crown. Just say the fucking word."

I've never been afraid of Arcturus or Bray. Arcturus is near twice my size in shifted form, but he's my friend. I have believed my entire life that he would never hurt me. And even though Bray is more prone to violence, he chooses his battles carefully. He has never once turned on his pack; to do so would be akin to committing suicide. "Knock it the fuck off." I puff my chest out as Bray comes closer, the warmth of his breath beating down on my face. "I'm trying to protect us."

"We can take any of them," Bray narrows his eyes at me. He's only a couple of inches taller than my 6'3", but he lords it over me like any big brother would. "The three of us together are as good as any pack ten times our size."

We used to say that to ourselves when we were younger. Our pack used to have six members, but as Arcturus came of age, we watched our numbers dwindle. Bray's brother was killed during a raid, a fact that only served to make him more ruthless as time wore on. Arcturus' brother left when it became clear that Arcturus' size would always overshadow his age and experience. He was older than Arcturus, but his little brother was bigger and tougher, and in the Forbidden Lands that made all the difference. We haven't heard from him since his departure and it's a topic we steer clear of. And Harleon? Well, we don't talk about what happened to him.

We have believed in ourselves wholeheartedly because no one else will. Other packs see us and think they can pick us off one by one, but it is *because* of our size that we're so closely bonded. Some days it feels like we share a brain; we always know what the others are thinking.

But we've grown since the days when we thought we could take on the world and live to tell the tale. We're smarter now, and we know our limits. "Bray, enough," I sigh.

His fists tighten at his sides, but after a few seconds, he backs down. With a huff, he returns to his sandwich on the counter. "She's the right girl, Fausto." Bray points his butter knife at me to accentuate his point. "She'll help us restore the Forbidden Lands. We've grown soft over the years, but not anymore. The districts will fear us again," he lowers his blunted weapon, "believe me."

I wish I could. I wish it were as easy as saying that Bray has a point. Once we bring back the blood of the queen that ruled over these lands with an iron fist, the wolves will flock back to us. They'll listen to Arcturus when he speaks. They'll follow the laws of his commanders, Bray and myself.

But it isn't that simple. As much as I wish it was, it isn't. People will ask questions and have doubts. We'll have to prove Elspeth's lineage over and over again. If she's truly as powerless as she claims, we'll have to find a way to use that to our advantage.

It isn't as simple as presenting her to the packs and claiming she's the long-lost granddaughter of the most fearsome wolf shifter to ever live in the Forbidden Lands. It is unfortunately much, much harder than that. And I don't know why Arcturus and Bray can't see that.

ELSPETH

The smell bowls me over. When Roth opens the door to the dungeons, I am hit in the face with the sour taste of filthy bodies and excrement. "Please, no," I fight against him, "don't make me go down there. I'll do whatever they want, I promise!" It's the exact opposite of what I just told myself I'd do.

Roth doesn't listen to my pleas, letting every fearful promise fall on his deaf ears as he takes me deeper into the bowels of the dungeon. "Do you know who's down here?"

I avert my eyes from the cells the second my foot is on the ground floor. One man looks severely bruised and beaten and the color of his skin turns my stomach. "Please take me back upstairs," I beg.

"The Kings' enemies. Men that have wronged

them. Witches that thought they could tame the wolves of the Forbidden Lands. Women that used their bodies to take advantage of the favors the Kings hand out." Roth jerks me toward him, causing my eyes to unjustly land on a suffering victim behind him. Her hair is matted and her eyes look wild, like a feral dog in captivity. "No one leaves the dungeon until they give the Kings what they want."

The feral woman laughs. If you could call the sound that escapes her lips laughter. It's a bone-dry chuckle that heaves from her lips like breath. "The Mad Kings."

Roth doesn't pay her any mind, but he turns to me and says, "They don't like to be called that. Refer to them only by their names or they'll make you regret it." I whimper as he leads me to a cell far from the cacophony of dying, angry prisoners. "You'll be safer over here. I recommend that you don't make friends."

He says this loud enough that it garners the attention of the two cells in front of my mine. A man and a woman lift their heads to take a look at me. "That's a pretty one," the man calls, "they'll take care of that in no time."

A shiver races down my spine as I'm forced inside the cell. Roth gives me a curious look as he shuts the door behind me with a dread-inducing clang. "I've known the Kings since they were little wolf pups that couldn't control their shifting. I was friends with their parents when they were still alive. They will test your fortitude, girl, but you will survive."

I can't keep from shaking. The temperature in the cell feels like it's dropped twenty degrees. "H-how do you know?" My teeth chatter together in fear, or maybe it's the cold.

Roth walks away and is gone for a couple of minutes. When he returns, he has an armful of blankets that he squeezes through the bars of my cell. "I've seen a lot of people come through the doors of this castle, during the Kings reign and during reigns before them, believe me when I say that I just know."

I don't know what that means, but I thank him for the blankets. They're scratchy and smell like mildew, but I wrap them around me one by one as Roth disappears. This time he doesn't return, leaving me in the ill-lit dungeon with my fears and the moans of other prisoners.

"Whatcha here for?" The woman across the hall asks. She presses her face into the bars and wraps her bony fingers around the metal.

I don't respond because I'm not sure. My father's words come back to me, but I can't hear them over the sound of her talking.

"I tried to kill Bray. Took a spin on his you-know-what first though." Her eyes are gaunt and sunken as if she hasn't eaten in a fortnight. "Nobody ever believes me," she exclaims when I don't respond. "I met him at a tavern, I did. I was going to kill him there, but he invited me back to the castle. No one ever comes back to the castle."

As she prattles on, I sink down onto the raised bed in the cell. It's six inches off the ground and it feels like the thin mattress is a sheer blanket draped over the concrete. Every movement feels like my bones are grinding against the hard surface. The exhaustion of the last few hours weighs heavily on my eyelids and as I lean against the wall to support my back, I close my eyes.

"Wake up!" The woman across the hall shouts. "You have to listen to me." Her eyes widen, giving her a strange look. "They are bad, bad men. They call them the Mad Kings," she rants. "Bray is mad. They are all mad. Mad. Mad. Mad."

I think she's slipping into delirium. She keeps whispering the word 'mad' as she pulls away from the cell bars and walks around her 7x7 space. Every few minutes, she laughs. I watch her step onto the mattress and trample over the already torn apart bedding. She's barefoot and her soles are blackened from the ground.

"Don't mind her," the man in the adjacent cell says in a bored voice. "She was tortured yesterday and she always gets a little loopy after a session with the Kings." He lays on his bed with his feet facing opposite my cell.

"T-torture?" I barely get the word out of my mouth. "They torture you?"

He tilts his head back until he can view me upside down. I see a book in his lap as he contorts his body. "They'll torture you, too. You best get used to that cell. No one leaves the dungeons alive."

Despite the three blankets Roth brought for me wrapped tightly around my shoulders, I grow even colder. There's a fourth blanket lying between me and the mattress, but I don't have the energy to force myself off the bed long enough to drape it over my body. Instead, I lie down on the sorry excuse for bedding and try to calm my fears by breathing deeply and counting to one hundred.

Somewhere between 57 and 58, my mind drifts from the repetitive process. A week ago I was in my own home, sleeping in my own bed. There were guards who kept me safe from attacks like this. There were maids that made sure every one of my needs were met. My parents spent hours with me every day teaching me about different herbs and plants and what their uses were. I foolishly thought that in two years' time, my father would marry me off to a nice man in the district and we'd be one happy family. My life seemed perfect.

Nothing could have prepared me for being kidnapped in the middle of the night. Nothing equipped me for the smell of unwashed bodies stained with blood and dirt. I couldn't have known what was going to happen to me a few days later and that's a terrifying realization. But no more terrifying than the realization that I've never been on my own before.

A song from my childhood pops into my head. The sound of my father's voice as he held me when I was sick rings loudly through my thoughts. *You are my sunshine, my only sunshine.* I drift off to memory. It's so vivid that it almost feels like he's here in the cell running his hands through my hair and holding me tight.

Everything will be better in the morning. It has to be.

ELSPETH

I don't know if I slept or just drifted in and out of nightmares, but I awaken to the sound of someone sliding a metal tray across the floor. My heart seizes in fear until I realize that it's food. The sound of people filling their bellies begins to pervade the dungeon. People chatter with one another about the morning's offering as I force myself upright.

My entire body aches. The mattress feels even thinner after lying on it for several hours. Everything from my shoulders to my tailbone hurts when I walk; I feel like I've prematurely aged thirty years.

The plate on the ground in front of my cell door looks edible enough. The main dish is probably oatmeal, otherwise, the pale color means there's something ripe on my tray. We've also been given a complimentary fruit cup and a cup of milk. It's as wholesome as school breakfast during your formative years.

I reach through the bars to set the cup of milk to the side. As much as I'd like a glass of water, if I touch those eight ounces of milk, I'll spend the rest of the day doubled over on the crude toilet installed in our cells. I'm not friends with dairy and this doesn't seem like the kind of place that will accommodate my needs with a Lactaid pill or some almond milk.

The rest of the tray I pull under the last bar. It's tall enough for the cup of milk to slide under, but there's no way a person could escape through this narrow passageway. The oatmeal is cold when I spoon it into my mouth, but it isn't bad. Whoever made the dish added a pinch of salt and some cinnamon. It could be worse; I could be eating bland oatmeal.

I can't remember the last time I had a fruit cup, but it hits the spot. I even drink down every last bit of the juices inside for hydration.

"You gonna drink that?" The guy across the hall asks. When I look up, I see him eyeing my forgotten cup of milk as he licks his lips.

"No?" I reach through the bars and grab the cup, pushing it as far as I can toward his cell. He's been here longer than I have, if he wants my milk, I'm happy to let him have it.

It's a struggle to get it to him though. At one point I watch him shove his foot through the bars to pull the cup closer with his toes. But after a few minutes, he slides it across the floor enough to grab it with his hands. "Your loss," he says as he downs it. "We won't get any water until lunch. *If* they give us lunch," he chuckles.

I drank the fruit juice, I remind myself. *And there's hydration in the food.* But my mouth is dry and my tongue feels thick; lunch feels like a long way off.

"You," a guard approaches without making a sound. His voice startles me and I jump away from the cell door. "Come with me." That's when I notice that he's staring at me. He waves his hand over the lock and the door starts to open. "Leave the blankets," he says with a sneer.

As I let them fall to the ground, I remember that I arrived here practically naked. Half of my nightgown is open on one side and the chunk taken out of my hem gives every prisoner an eyeful of my thigh. I do my best to clothe myself by holding the bits of fabric together while trying to pull it down, but it doesn't help much.

This time when I walk through the dungeon hallway, the lights are brighter. I get a better view of my fellow prisoners and I see them in various states of insanity. But one thing is certain about all of them: each wears a crudely made metal collar around their neck.

"Hurry up," the guard growls when he notices me lingering.

I quicken my pace, afraid that if I stop any longer, he'll hit me. The guard seems like the type to abuse his prisoners. He has thick, meaty hands and three rings on his left. One punch to the face and he could knock out half my teeth.

When we reach the top, the guard stops long enough to grab me by the arm. Unfortunately, it's the arm holding my gown together. I'm forced to release the fabric and the cool morning air hits my body. Goose pimples coat my flesh as he leads me through a series of hallways and up a couple more staircases. He doesn't say anything to me, but I catch him leering at the opening in my gown.

We reach another guard several minutes later, this one stands before two large floor-to-ceiling wood doors. I'm traded from one guard to the next without an exchange of words. Then the doors open up and I'm forced forward. "Prisoner 712, your grace." The guard leads me a few more feet before foisting me forward.

I stumble from the shove but manage to catch myself before I lose my footing and hit the ground. In front of me are the Mad Kings, behind me the doors are closing. I want to make a run for it, but fear keeps me rooted to my spot.

"Good morning, Elspeth," Arcturus greets me solemnly. He sits in the largest, most ornate chair of the three. He doesn't wear a crown, but he speaks with all the authority of the person in charge. "I'd like to apologize for my man. We have never had royal prisoners before."

I right myself before him, straightening my back and trying to look unfazed. "Why am I here?"

He exchanges a glance with Bray and Fausto, a smile dancing on his lips a few moments later. "Why do you *think* you're here?"

I can't hide the exasperation in my sigh when he asks that question. I want to shout at him that I don't know why he infiltrated my house in the middle of the night and stole me from my bedroom, but I'm afraid that if I raise my voice, something worse will happen to me than a few hours on a hard, concrete cot. "I'm not sure," I tell him honestly. "I-I think it has something to do with my father though." It's an educated guess based on what they said last night. They blamed him for hiding me away, but I don't know what I was supposedly hidden from.

Arcturus nods his head slowly. "That is almost correct. Sources tell me that your father made it through the night. Though it's of little comfort to me," he rolls his eyes, "it might be meaningful to you."

I didn't know I was holding in so much tension until I breathe a sigh of relief and feel half my muscles unclench. "Thank you." Should I ask what they did to him? If he was badly injured? He must have been if they thought he wouldn't survive the night.

"Fausto, would you do the honors?" Arcturus isn't

talking to me anymore. He turns his head to the right and nods at his friend.

I watch the man get out of his seat and bound across the floor toward me. I take a step backward in fear before he tells me to knock it off. "I just need a taste of your blood." His tone is bored, but the look in his eyes is salacious.

He reaches me before I have enough time to turn on my heel and make a break for the door, but all he does is grab my wrist. With his other hand, he frees a knife from his pocket and brings it to my delicate flesh. "This will sting for a few seconds, but we need to make sure you are who you say you are."

Before I have a chance to argue, the knife makes a small, 1-inch slit beneath my palm. I hiss from the pain and try to pull away, but Fausto is stronger than I am. As blood pools from the cut, he brings my wrist up to his lips. In a way far more sensitive than I ever believed him capable of, Fausto drags his tongue across the open wound.

Seconds pass and it feels like an eternity, but eventually, Fausto closes his knife and shoves it back into his pocket. He reaches into another and procures a bandage. As he applies it tenderly, he avoids making eye contact. "It's her," he says gruffly when the bandage is firmly in place. He whispers a thank you to me and for a fleeting moment, I see pleasure in his gaze. Fausto releases my wrist and I bring it firmly into my body, holding my wounded arm close. But nothing more happens. He turns and walks back to his seat, a little less bounce in his step than before.

"With that out of the way, let's discuss." Arcturus claps his hands together in delight. "Now, what's this nonsense about you being a witch?"

ARCTURUS

lspeth's painstaking explanation of her
father's lies makes my blood boil. Nothing
would delight me more than shifting into
my wolf form and returning to the Cersei district to
finish the job Bray started last night.

"You never thought it was strange that two shifters
birthed a witch?" Fausto asks unbelievingly. "That's
not even possible. Even if somewhere in your family
tree a shifter and a witch crossbred, there's no way
that it would have been passed down to you."

She shrugs her shoulders looking even smaller
than her delicate 5'3" frame.

Bray presses his fingers to his temples and asks
what she thought her father was protecting her from
with all those guards. "You couldn't have truly
believed the shifters in the Forbidden Lands would

come in the night and steal you away for no reason," he says with a scoff.

"But didn't you?" Elspeth asks. Immediately, I can see the regret on her face. Her cheeks turn a vibrant shade of red and she starts to backpedal. "I mean, I guess I don't understand why I'm here. You say that my father lied to me, that I'm a-a shifter like my parents, but there are people born without magic and abilities. Maybe you thought you were taking me because of my race, but it could have been a mistake. I'm not a shifter at all and you don't need actually need me."

If her face wasn't so sweet and innocent, I'd think she was acting, trying to put us off the scent. But Elspeth looks genuinely terrified. Every new revelation that Fausto and Bray share with her makes her eyes widen with realization. I think she's truly blameless in all of this.

"You have the blood of your ancestors," Fausto tells her after a few minutes. "I could taste it running through your veins. You're not a witch, you're not magicless, you're a shifter, Elspeth."

"No," she shakes her head, "no, I'm not." Elspeth looks frustrated with the three of us. Her eyes beg and plead for us to understand. That's when I realize how far the depth of her father's lies goes. She has been disillusioned in her short twenty years of life and one night isn't going to undo the brainwashing.

I hold my hand up to stop the other two from speaking. Elspeth needs to know the history of our land. If she understands where she came from, she'll understand why we brought her here. Bray and Fausto telling her over and over again that she's been lied to and had her magic suppressed will only make her angrier.

"Elspeth," I clear my throat, "the Forbidden Lands have been inhabited for more than five centuries. The woman that brought the forgotten and banned shifters together was one of the most fearsome wolves to ever exist. For generations, her blood ran through the veins of her heirs. The crown always passed from one Nikae woman to the next and when she chose her pack, they would reign over the Forbidden Lands until the throne passed to the next heir."

The children of Meira'mor go to school and learn about the history of their world and the humans', but the children of the Forbidden Lands learn about the wars we fought for our freedom and the women that led us to victory. I can remember the last ten rulers of the land, all of them born with Nikae blood. I can recite our historical texts regarding the way they brought the packs together and created a community. Everything changed after Alize Nikae was taken, but I remember the old ways.

"60 years ago, your grandfather crossed onto our land and kidnapped our queen. In a show of strength for the mainlanders, he forced her to marry him and bred her like a prized racehorse." The day our teacher told us about Alize's capture, she cried. "Our predecessors refused to travel to the mainlands and save her. Alize was their heart and soul and without her, they couldn't see a way forward."

In some ways, that mindset still exists. I have ruled over these lands for a decade and made no more progress than the pack before me. "But our queen's blood runs through your veins, Elspeth. You are a direct descendent of the last queen."

Elspeth's mouth parts in protest. "I'm not," she swears quickly, "honest. I'm a witch. I'm a healer of some kind." Her cries fall on deaf ears. "I'm not a shifter or a wolf or anything at all. There's nothing special about me, I promise."

It occurs to me that the woman standing in front of us will not lead an army into battle, not anytime soon, but there's something about her that draws me like a moth to the flame. Her innocence is infectious and it makes me want to take her in my arms and swear that she'll never be hurt again. But I cannot give in to those feelings, not while she hasn't embraced her true nature.

"Did you know that diamonds do not start out flawless and polished?" Elspeth's eyebrows form a downward-facing arrow as she stares at me. "Diamonds start out like you, as nothing special. But when enough force and pressure is applied, they become precious and rare."

I get out of my chair and walk over to the frightened young woman before me. She meets my eyes when I grab her chin and force her to look up at me. "You are a diamond, Elspeth, and we are the pressure. You *will* be ours. You *will* marry us. You *will* give us children. Because you belong in the Forbidden Lands, atop that seat," I point behind me at the ostentatious chair I just arose from. "And no matter what it takes, we will make you strong enough to climb those stairs and embrace the rule that your ancestors imparted upon you. Do I make myself clear?"

Her bottom lip trembles and her gorgeous, dark eyes cloud with horror. She is a mess of emotions as I feel her slick, hot tears slide down her cheeks and land on my fingers. "I didn't ask for this. I don't want this," she breathes.

I dig my fingers into her jaw until I hear her gasp in pain. "It doesn't matter; this is your mantle to take up now. You will learn, Elspeth, and you *will* prevail. I don't care what we have to do to make it happen."

Elspeth's legs turn wobbly beneath her and I release my grip on her chin only to watch her fall. Her cries become a blubbering mess as she tries to plead with us to let her go and find a new queen.

I walk back to my chair and call for the guard. "Take her back to the dungeons," I order. "Have her clothed and make sure that it's expressed to all the prison guards that she is not to be touched. No matter what rules she breaks, her misdeeds are to be brought directly to us. If anyone lays a finger on her without our approval, they'll find themselves in a cell right beside her."

The guard nods his head before prying Elspeth off the ground. He whispers a few words in her ear and she manages to stand on her own, but he keeps a firm grip on her bicep while he leads her out of the room.

"Do you think she has it in her to lead?" Fausto asks after the doors shut.

"If her display of tears has anything to say about it, no, she will never be strong enough. But she *is* a Nikae." I cling to her bloodline like a dying man clings to life. All I can do is hope that she will rise to the occasion. It will take some convincing, but they don't call us the Mad Kings for nothing. If anyone can persuade a woman to power, it's us.

ELSPETH

Every step I take toward the dungeon feels like another twenty-pound weight is added to my feet. By the time we reach the final staircase, I feel like I'm encased in concrete. "You can let me go," I beg the guard, "just say that I escaped. Tell them that you lost me when I was going to the bathroom or something."

The guard doesn't even look at me twice. When I won't walk down the stairs on my own, he drags me. "If I lose you, I'll wind up in a cell myself. Better you down here than me."

When we reach the ground floor and the smell of human waste hits me square in the face once more, the guard hands me back to the man that delivered me upstairs. "She's to be clothed and taken care of. If she falls out of line, report it immediately to the Kings. They don't want her touched."

The dungeon guard gives me a glare and a sneer. "What's so special about this one? She a better whore than the other girls they've had ride their cocks?"

My cheeks turn hot with shame as I feast my eyes on the ground. I've never been so cruelly humbled like this before. Even when I was younger and my father told me in no uncertain terms that I had failed to generate any pure magic or abilities, at least I could accept his instruction because I knew that it was true. This is so absurd that it turns my stomach sour.

The King's guard shrugs his shoulders in response. "I don't know. It looks like they didn't torture her. I bet she's taking them all at once." They share a laugh and a high five while I stand there wondering if that's what my future will entail. Arcturus said that they want me to have their babies. That will mean spreading my legs for them, something I've never done for anyone else before.

When the two guards are finished making fun of me, I'm led back to my cell. "Why you ain't got no collar?" The guard asks as we stop in front of the bars of my empty prison.

I look up at him, confused. Didn't *he* put the collars on the prisoners? "I-I don't know."

He narrows his eyes at me before opening the door and shoving me inside. "I'm gonna get you a collar, girl." He says it like it's a promise and I'm confused, but before I can ask him what the collars do, he's walking back to his post while grumbling under his breath about pretty girls getting away with murder.

"They collar us like dogs," the woman from across the way begins. She presses her face against the bars as her hands scratch at the metal around her neck. "Collars," she whispers, "bad collars. Collars for bad dogs. We're bad dogs."

"Enough, Bilia," the man in the cell next to her groans. "Fucking hell. I wish they'd just kill her already," he sighs as he raises from his bed to look in my direction. "I'm sick of her rambling the week after they've had a session with her. She's normal for three days before she's called back up there and tortured again. It's never-fucking-ending."

I'm startled by his anger. Just a little bit ago he seemed easygoing, but now he's on edge. I guess that's the price you pay when you're housed in a concrete square all day. "Do they torture you?" I remember Roth's words from last night. *I recommend that you don't make friends.* But I have nothing else to do besides ask questions and get comfortable.

The man shrugs his shoulders. Though I can see his eyes, he doesn't look directly at me. Instead, his blue gaze dances across my cell from wall to wall, occasionally landing on me for no more than a few seconds before flitting away. "When they're angry and need a punching bag, they call any of us. They start with the prisoners on that side of the dungeon first," he gestures with his head toward the cells I haven't seen yet. "Then, women. They love to torture women. Maybe your screams are more entertaining. Maybe they just like seeing your bodies ripped apart. There's a woman with no arm over there." The man once again points his chin away from us. "She cried for a week. I don't know why they didn't kill her."

I feel sick and the shivering returns. Wasn't I supposed to be properly clothed? I'm still walking around in a tattered nightgown. No matter. I don't think an appropriate pair of pants and a shirt would keep me from being chilled to the bone by fear.

I grab the blankets I shed before I left and start to wrap them around me again. If I used them as a mattress topper, maybe my body wouldn't hurt so much when I sat down, but I desperately need them for warmth instead.

"Why *don't* you have a collar?" The man asks curiously. His eyes are now focused on the spot where my feet touch the ground.

I shrug my shoulders feeling as unaware as him. The Mad Kings might have explained why I'm here, but I still don't understand *why* I'm here. "I don't know. Why do *you* have a collar?"

He fingers the metal around his throat and when I narrow my eyes to get a better look, I can see scratch marks above and below the thick metal. "I've heard they're like the collars from the Meira'mor asylums. They inhibit all magic. I was a demon once," he says with a heaving sigh, "I'm just Rigo now."

"I'm just Elspeth," I return. "I wasn't anything before."

For the first time since I arrived a few hours ago, he makes eye contact with me. His gaze is a startling blue. "You are already powerless," he says in a matter-of-fact tone.

It occurs to me that I've been powerless all my life; no one has ever needed a collar to keep me in line. "I guess so, Rigo."

It takes him a few minutes to respond. Though he's more put together than Bilia in the cell next to him, he still struggles to find the right words. It's as if he has to scour his memory for understanding of the English language. "They must want you for something else then," he finally says in a whisper. "You have hurt them or you have something they want. That's the only reason we're all here." Rigo maintains eye contact when he mutters, "They only keep us here if we hurt them or if we have something they want." He rambles, but he's right.

I pull the blankets around me tighter, hoping that the guard arrives soon with a warmer pair of clothes. "What if I can't give them what they want?"

My question is followed by silence, then the sound

of movement. Rigo makes himself comfortable on his bed again and grabs his book. This time his feet face me and I can see the cover. There are no words, which only makes me more curious about what he's reading. "Then you die," Rigo says after he's flipped through a couple of pages.

My only options can't be mother of wolves or dead; I'm not prepared for either outcome.

ELSPETH

I don't know if the guards are trying to freeze me out or if they don't care about the Mad Kings' wishes. I sit in my cell for hours, wrapped up in my blankets waiting for clothes. Goosebumps feel like they're just part of my skin now. The blankets I have almost seem to lose their warmth after a while.

Rigo occasionally asks a question, never turning back to look at me. *Who are you? Where are you from? Do you know what they want from you? Why are you here? What can you do? Do you have any magic? Is that why you aren't wearing a collar?*

Bilia rocks back and forth in her bed. She rambles incessantly under her breath and occasionally yells her insanity aloud. I never know what to say or do in response.

I lie down on my cot and wish there was a clock. I

scarf down the offerings that they call lunch. A sandwich of only bread and cheese. The same cup from
earlier, but this time filled with water. A bundle of
celery and carrots that hardly crunch when I bite into
them. It isn't the most nutritious lunch, but it does the
trick. My mom used to say the best seasoning is
hunger, but even hunger doesn't make the celery taste
like it's fresh.

I wait for the Mad Kings to call me. Rigo says that
it will happen at any moment. "If you know that they
want something from you, then you know that you're
gonna get out of here eventually. Well, at least get up
to the castle. I don't know if you'll ever get out of
here."

His belief that I'll never leave is what drags me
under. Sometimes, as I'm laying on my bed staring at
the ceiling, I wonder what's going on at home. Is my
father searching for me? Is my mother crying her eyes
out? Do any of them care that I am gone at all? I've
always felt like a burden on my parents. Maybe they're
happy that I'm gone now. Maybe this is what they've
secretly wished for since the day they found out that I
couldn't produce any magic.

We are served dinner as the sun starts to set. I'm
given another cup of water for my troubles alongside a
piece of meat that looks very suspicious. A scoop of
peas and carrots swim in their own water in the side
dish. If it's all supposed to be warm, then the cook

failed his job. The food arrives in various stages of lukewarm, taking away from what little taste the food has.

Luckily, dinner is well-salted. Despite not knowing what kind of meat I am eating, it doesn't taste half bad. I hate the texture of peas, but since they're all that I have, I eat them happily.

Rigo asks if I'm going to eat everything, hopeful that he'll get a little something extra the way he did at breakfast time. I don't respond. We are not friends; we are prisoners that share a hallway.

But the next morning, he leaves before breakfast. The guard comes and says that he is to see the Mad Kings. The tall, angry-looking guard wears a smirk on his lips that says he can't wait to see what the Kings do this time. Rigo clenches his jaw and tries not to make a fuss, but I can see him shaking with fear as the guard drags him away.

When he returns, he is quieter than before. New bruises have bloomed on his body. His hair is now shaved off. Blood drips from his toenails but not for long. The guard returns a short while later with a bandage for his foot. I keep waiting for the guard to come back with the clothes the Mad Kings said that I could wear, but he never does.

I make it through my second day with nothing but my thoughts and blankets. And the ramblings of Bilia, which are slowly becoming saner. For the first time since I arrived, Rigo is silent. He doesn't read his book, he just stares at the wall. His pristine white bandage slowly becomes dingier with every walk from his bed to the toilet. Between the two of them, it terrifies me to think about what will happen when the guard takes me upstairs next. But I'd be lying if I said I didn't want it to happen.

I want to plead my case to the Kings. I want to explain to them that I can't do this. I'm not the Queen that they're searching for. I've never led anything in my life, let alone an outlying district of misfit shifters.

After two straight days of being in my cell, I am unprepared for the guard's arrival. He shows up with a sneer and some clothes. "Put these on," he demands gruffly before throwing the swathes of fabric at me through the bars.

I grab my new outfit off the floor and shed my blankets. With my back to the guard, Rigo, and Bilia, I slip out of my nightgown and into a soft pair of pants and a long sleeve shirt. It feels like an eternity since I last wore something this comfortable.

The guard is opening the door when I turn back around. He ushers me forward and grabs my bicep like he did a couple of days before. "The Kings want to see you," he says with a growl. Then he drags me through the hallway of the prison as if I can't walk on my own two feet.

Would it be wrong to be thankful? To be excited to

go upstairs? I have had nothing but time to think about the offer that the Kings proposed. They can't turn me into what they want me to be. I cannot be the fearsome wolf-shifting leader that they want me to be. If I tell them that, will they let me go or let me rot in the dungeons below until I die?

The weather must be nice today because we pass several open windows when the guard reaches the ground floor. I wish we could open a few windows in the dungeon; it might help get rid of the smell. I've learned in my short time here that it isn't the people causing the stench, it is the outdated equipment that they provide for us. Half the time the toilet doesn't flush. Sometimes I hear swearing and cursing from the other side of the dungeon as somebody flushes the toilet and their cell is flooded. Luckily, mine hasn't done that yet. But yesterday I watched as Bilia's backed up and threatened to overflow. It took hours before the water receded.

"Do you like being here?" I ask the guard. "Is this what you've always dreamed of doing?" If I can make friends with the guard, perhaps it could lead to an escape.

The guard looks at me as if I am insane. "What do you mean *dreamed of* doing?" He scuffs as he turns down another hall and leads me up a flight of stairs. "This isn't the mainlands. We do what is required of us here in the Forbidden Lands. For me, that means taking care of the Kings' prisoners. That includes taking care of you." He gives me a once over, his eyes trailing from my head to my toes, and his nose wrinkles in disgust when he reaches the floor. "I don't know what the Kings see in you, but it's more than I do. You look like a strong storm could blow you away. You are a waif of a woman."

He dumps me in front of the throne room. The guard standing before the doors nods his head approvingly. "I see that you were clothed," he comments, "though I don't know who's clothes those are. They probably belong to a dead person." The way he says it is filled with malice and delight as if imagining me wearing the clothes someone else died in is a hilarious thought.

I never realized that the clothes I'd be given might have come from someone's cold, dead body. Suddenly everything feels itchy. I want to tear off these rags and jump back into my nightgown. I'd rather be partially clothed than wear someone's last outfit.

"The Mad Kings will see you now," the guard announces as he opens the doors and ushers me through.

BRAY

It was Arcturus' idea to let her sit in the cell for two days. "It'll do her some good," he said with a shrug. "She needs time to think about all of this."

I didn't necessarily see it that way, but I wasn't going to argue. I was concerned by the way she broke down at the end of our first conversation. If she couldn't handle a little tough love, what made me certain that she'd lead the Forbidden Lands one day? But maybe Arcturus was right. If she was given time to come to terms with her future, maybe she'd rise to the occasion. If diamonds are pressed to polish and prestige, she could be pressed to her queenly duties.

"I'm having the guard bring Elspeth up shortly," Arcturus breaks the silence at the breakfast table.

Fausto is picking at his eggs but perks up when he

hears the announcement. "Really?" His eyebrows raise into his hairline. "The prisoner from yesterday reported that she still hadn't moved. Do you think it's time?"

The prisoner across the hallway from Elspeth, Rodrigo Dawse, was brought in to answer how she was doing. He said that she seemed fine enough, but she was very quiet. His information was lacking and therefore it bored Arcturus. Every toenail on Rodrigo's right foot was removed until the floor was stained with his blood and he couldn't put any weight on it. "Next time, bring me better answers," Arcturus threatened, "or worse will happen."

"If she isn't ready, then she'll face her own punishment." Arcturus grabs the napkin from his lap and uses it to daintily clean up his face. "She needs to become accustomed to being around us, Fausto. If she can be trained, she can be used. If we have to break her first, so be it."

Delight roars in my chest. I have wanted to put my hands on Elspeth since the day we found out that she was Alize's granddaughter. My motivation has been half lust and half genetic predisposition. I come from a line of shifters that have been tied to the Nikae bloodline before. I yearn for her in an animalistic, primal sort of way.

When Arcturus rises from his chair, Fausto and I are quick to follow. He leads us to the throne room and tells the guard that a prisoner will be arriving soon. We make ourselves comfortable and wait.

Elspeth's arrival is curious for a number of reasons. She wears a cream-colored sweatsuit that has every inch of her body covered. The dark locks that I long to press my face into are matted from sleep and lack of care. There are hollows beneath her eyes, darkened with exhaustion and fear. It's only been two days, but it looks like she's already losing touch with reality.

As she stands before us, she sways a bit. She has the look of men we've spent months torturing. We haven't put a finger on her, yet Elspeth looks depleted. "I can't do this," she says in a dead voice. "I'm not cut out for this."

A lesser man would break. He would free Elspeth from the dungeon and put her in the lap of luxury. A soft bed, pretty dresses, and all the food and water she could ask for. But Arcturus is not a lesser man; he is the first point of the crown. "Tell me how you use echinacea," he demands instead.

Elspeth lifts her eyes from the floor to look at Arcturus unbelievingly. Her brow furrows in confusion before she slowly answers him. "We use it for wound healing. If someone is too weak to stay in their shifted form long enough to heal, the leaves are spliced and placed on their cuts. Most of the time though, we use it for colds and sicknesses. The liquid is extracted from the root and placed in a tea made with peppermint, rosemary, and thyme. Among other herbs and plants, depending on what we can find," she adds at the last second.

Arcturus nods his head as she speaks. As far as I know, he knows nothing about the healing properties of a plant or an herb. Unless he's done some research in the last two days, she could be talking out of her ass and he wouldn't know the difference. "How did you learn that?" He asks when she finishes.

She blinks at him several times before looking to Fausto and then across the room to me. Her mouth is open, poised to speak, but she doesn't say anything for many long moments. "I was taught by witches in my father's employ."

"Ah, so you *can* be taught," Arcturus says with a lascivious smile.

Elspeth's frown deepens. She tries to understand what this all means, but either exhaustion has taken its toll or she simply doesn't get it. "Yes?" She questions. "I suppose."

He drums his fingers on the armrest of his throne; they make a soft tap as the pads come in contact with the iron. "We want to teach you to shift, Elspeth. That is your natural gift, borne to you by the gods upon your conception. It is who you are deep down and it is the greatest gift you could have."

Her frown turns into frustration. I watch her mouth snap close and her jaw tighten as she grinds her teeth together. "When will you listen to me?" She begs. "I am not a shifter. My parents tried when I was young, but I didn't have the ability. You can't force me to shift."

Arcturus transforms unexpectedly. He jumps off of his throne and lunges at Elspeth. In mid-air, he shifts into his wolfish form. He grows before our very eyes, becoming a large, snarling Canis lupus.

Elspeth screams and falls to the floor. She tries to scurry away from him, but he's on top of her in a second. He gnashes his teeth only inches from her neck, causing her to beg for her life. Then slowly, he drags his tongue along the curve of the only skin she has bared. A long trail of saliva curves around her throat as he takes her in. From this distance, I see tears staining her face.

"He won't hurt you." I get up from my chair and walk a little closer, desperate to be as near to this woman as Arcturus is. "Not much, anyway," I add with a chuckle. As I crouch down beside the two of them, I run my finger across her cheek. "You have two choices, Elspeth. You can do what we ask you to or," I pause, popping my thumb between her lips, "you can stay in the dungeon until you breathe your last breath."

Her skin is soft beneath the filth and grime from her prison cell. There is still innocence in her gaze. "What we're doing isn't wrong, it's necessary. And if you don't get your act together soon, Arc might not stop at licking this pretty little throat. He might be tempted to take a chunk out, maybe two. Who knows?"

Elspeth's tears begin anew but her whimpers are silenced by my thumb in her mouth. Seeing her sweet, plump little lips wrapped around my digit makes me wish it was something else she was sucking on.

"Forget all that healer witch nonsense, okay?" I lean down to press my lips to her forehead before regrettably having to pull away. I already miss the warmth of her mouth around my thumb. "We're going to teach you to shift, princess, and you're going to like it."

Both Arcturus and I back away from her. She remains frozen in her spot on the ground, eyes wide with fright. As my compatriot shifts back to his human form, the glint of hunger in his eyes only intensifies. "You taste superb, darling," he smirks, "I can't wait to taste you everywhere else."

I'm jealous of him, of Fausto, too. They've both had an intimate moment with Elspeth. But I am patient, at least in these matters. When my moment with Elspeth comes, it will be glorious. "Get up," I nod my head at her, "it's time to begin your training."

ELSPETH

"Just visualize it," Arcturus growls. He stands behind me, his large, muscular body reflecting heat onto mine. "Imagine yourself as a wolf," he says more calmly. "Imagine the length of your body, the fur on your belly, the sharpness of your teeth," his words sound like poetry but cut me like a knife. He takes a step closer and I feel him press against me from behind as he comes even closer. The outline of his manhood against my backside makes my cheeks pink with embarrassment. "You are not Elspeth. You are not in this body any longer."

All this imagining is tiring me out. I'm exhausted from the two nights of broken sleep I've gotten by lying on a concrete cot. But I summon what's left of my energy to do as he instructs.

I think about all of the shifters I've met in my day.

My father: a black wolf with a white spot on his nose shaped like Africa. My mother: dark gray with strands of silver weaved through her mane. My brothers: twin light gray wolves that you can only tell apart by the color of their eyes. There are dozens of wolf shifters in the Cersei district I can visualize.

I take a deep breath and shut out the world, trying to do as Arcturus commands. *I am a wolf. I am graceful. I am vicious.* I can see it in my mind now, a fuzzy image of what I'm supposed to transform into. "What now?" I breathe, afraid that if I say too much, the image will disappear. "What do I do after I visualize it?"

Arcturus raises his hand to the place where my hip curves into my waistline. The warmth of his fingers on my body sends of shiver down my spine. "Now, imagine shifting."

Frustration fills me and I want to scream at him. *I don't know what that means! I don't know how to do that!* Shifting is not something that I've ever been taught. I remember my father trying to show me when I was five. I remember my mother gently taking the reins when I turned ten. When I hadn't successfully shifted by my fifteenth birthday, both of them quietly resigned from the task and allowed me to learn other practical abilities.

I pull away from Arcturus and his hand falls back to his side. "This is useless," I announce as I turn to face him. In the distance sits Bray and Fausto, both watching with curious eyes as we attempt the impossible. "My parents tried to do this for years and it never worked. I never shifted. I don't know what to imagine because I can't conceptualize what that looks or feels like."

I expect another angry outburst from Arcturus. He steps toward me and his tall, looming figure makes me feel three inches tall. "It's different for everyone," he admits after a few moments. The tone of his voice becomes more intimate. "Bray, what does it feel like to you?"

Bray rises from his chair and trots over to the two of us. He walks around Arcturus and me as if he's examining a crime scene. "It feels like all of the energy in the world is suddenly in my veins. It feels like I can do anything."

Following suit, Fausto lazily walks over and adds his two cents. "The first time I ever shifted, it felt like I was waking up for the first time in my life. Everything was better. Everything *is* better," he corrects quickly. "Colors are sharper. Smells are stronger. My body is indestructible."

As Bray and Fausto circle me like sharks, I look up to meet Arcturus' dark gaze. "Most people are not taught to shift, Elspeth." There is a frown poised on his features. "For 98% of us, it comes naturally. Sort of like breathing. But I suspect that your father didn't nurture your natural gifts. He would have known that you were Alize Nikae's granddaughter and he would have presumed the best way to keep you safe was to stifle your magic."

"But I've never heard that name before," I tell him with a pained expression. "My dad never talked about the Forbidden Lands unless he was warning me to stay far away from them. Neither did my mom. Grandma never said anything about living out here or being kidnapped."

Arcturus tilts his head a fraction to the left as his brow deepens with confusion. "You met your grandmother? You met Alize?"

I knew he was going to ask that and I kick myself for bringing it up. "Yes," I admit carefully, "but she is a very happy woman. She loves my grandfather and they're *happy* together. That's why I'm not sure that you've got the right person. My grandma's name is Alysin and she has been madly in love with my grandpa since the two of them ran away together and got married."

"Alysin," Fausto drops the name with disdain. "You don't think that bears a semblance to the name Alize?"

My head starts to throb and I reach up to press my fingers against my temples to staunch the oncoming pain. "I guess," I groan, "but that could just be a coincidence. You said that my grandpa came and kidnapped her, right? But they said that they ran away together. That doesn't match your story at all."

I haven't learned my lesson. Despite Arcturus transforming before my eyes and dragging his thick, wet tongue across my neck with his teeth only millimeters away, I am stubborn. I can't conform to their requests and it's my downfall.

Fausto lunges at me from behind and grabs my wrist. He drags my arm up the center of my back, twisting it so hard that I jerk forward to try and escape the pain. "When will you learn?" He hisses in my ear. "We did not take you from the Cersei district on a whim. We did our due diligence to make sure that you were Alize's granddaughter. Just because she changed her name to Alysin and claims some disgusting love story with your grandpa doesn't mean it's true."

The pain is blinding. The smallest tug on my arm sends another throbbing jolt through my body. "You're right," I say between gritted teeth. I'd tell them anything they want to hear.

Fausto pulls my arm a little harder until white lightning stretches across my vision. "Say it like you mean it."

"You're going to break her arm," Bray says a few feet away. His tone is bored and when I look at him, his arms are crossed in disinterest.

I grind my teeth together and brace myself for the crack, but it doesn't come. Fausto simply holds me at this angle, dangling me above the ground as he waits for me to give him what he wants. "My grandmother is Alize," I whisper. I can't summon the energy to speak any louder. All of my strength is going into keeping myself aloft so my arm doesn't break.

But the effort is useless. Seconds later, my shoulder dislocates and the pain is exquisite. Fausto releases me and I hit the ground with a thud. The cool stone feels like heaven on my sweating brow. It's almost enough to take my mind off the pain.

Almost.

ELSPETH

I stare at my limp arm like a third-party viewer. It is visibly deformed as a chunk of my shoulder juts backward in a sickening sort of way. I reach up to press the knot on my shoulder and scream in pain.

"I guess that's better than a break," Bray announces as he kneels down beside me. "But let the record show that I told you so." He glares up at Fausto.

Arcturus mimics Bray's action and kneels in front of me. He focuses on the bone-shaped knot formed by my shoulder being out of place. "We could take her to the doctor," he says wistfully, "or we can take care of it ourselves."

I barely have enough time to register his hands coming toward me when black spots fill my vision as he maneuvers the bone back into place. A wave of nausea washes over me. I can't swallow down the vomit fast enough and it winds up in my lap and splattered across Arcturus. My manners prevail and I apologize before I even reach up to wipe away the spittle on my bottom lip.

"You're cleaning this up," Arcturus says to Fausto as he gets to his feet. "You should have fucking known that you were going to seriously injure her with that move. You fucking imbecile. I'm covered in vomit." *I'm* covered in vomit; Arcturus just looks like he was hit by the backsplash, but I'm not going to correct him.

Fausto scoffs as he reaches down to grab my good arm. He slowly helps me to my feet with a glare on his face. "Boo-fucking-hoo," he rolls his eyes. "C'mon, Bray, let's get her cleaned up."

Arcturus is stripping down in the throne room. I catch a glimpse of his body before the two men escort me through the door. He has a six-pack of perfect abs and a tan that makes me envious, but scars crisscross over his chest and torso. "Make sure she goes back to the dungeon when you're done playing doctor!" His yell follows us into the hallway.

Surprisingly, despite his earlier act, Fausto is gentle with me. He cradles me around the waist and helps me down the first flight of stairs. Instead of heading down the usual hallway that leads back to the dungeon, he directs me away from the second staircase.

"You think the doc will be awake?" Bray asks as he stops in front of a door.

Fausto shrugs his shoulders. "He works for us, not the other way around. If he isn't awake, he's going to be now." He reaches forward to bang on the wooden door. "Open up, Levar!"

Levar arrives three seconds later. He's an older man only a few inches taller than me. He looks from Bray to Fausto and glares when he sees me. "Did you try to kill the poor girl?" He accuses as he ushers us inside. "She looks half dead."

I feel half dead, or maybe that's just the pain talking. Not to mention the vomit smearing the sweatsuit that I just got. It's a pity; I was just coming around to wearing a dead person's final outfit.

"Her shoulder was dislocated." Fausto escorts me to a chair and helps me sit down. "Arc relocated it. It was my doing but it wasn't intentional."

Could have fooled me. I would have sworn that he was going to break my arm in two at any moment. The only reason he didn't was because my shoulder failed me first. "I'm fine." My voice sounds weak.

Levar shakes his head at the two shifters that brought me here. "This shirt has to go," he says after a few moments. "I need to X-ray her arm to make sure you buffoons didn't do any permanent damage. And it's covered in vomit." He wrinkles his nose in disgust.

"I'm not wearing anything under here," I protest

quickly. I also can't lift my arm. Arcturus might have relocated my shoulder, but it feels like a stranger appended a new arm to my body that I have no control over.

The doctor leaves through a door in the corner of the room and when he returns, he's holding a towel. "Use that to cover up, miss. I need to see the shoulder."

When it becomes painfully clear that I can't help them remove the shirt, Bray and Fausto maneuver me while Levar cuts it off. I close my eyes in embarrassment and hold the towel close to my chest.

Levar's hands are warm when he reaches out to touch my shoulder. He starts to whisper a few words under his breath that I can't make out. A flood of frost fills my pained appendage as he mumbles his incantation. "It doesn't seem like anything is broken," Levar announces after a few more seconds. "But I want to put her in a sling to immobilize the shoulder while it heals. I'm also going to prescribe some pain relievers."

Bray clears his throat loudly and all eyes turn to him. "She's a prisoner, Levar."

He raises an eyebrow in questioning and when no response comes, he merely asks, "So?"

The doctor's reply catches Bray off guard. He stares at Levar and then looks over to me. I feel his eyes caressing the bare skin on my belly. "Fine, but I'll be the one to dispense the meds. I don't want you to give her a bottle of muscle relaxers and she swallow the whole damn thing after lights out."

Levar snorts and busies himself with looking through a large pantry full of medication. He has everything from traditional meds to books on how to cure cancerous growths. "You wouldn't want your captive to kill herself before you get the chance to do it," he says disrespectfully.

"Listen," Fausto approaches the doctor with a growl, "if you knew who you were speaking to, you'd do so with more respect."

The doctor feigns innocence when he turns with a bottle in hand. "I'm talking to the Kings, aren't I? How much more respect can I give you?"

It's a tense few moments as the two stare at one another. Despite being significantly shorter than Fausto, Levar doesn't cower before him. "Get me another set of clothes for her," Fausto demands.

"As you wish," Levar replies with a smile. He walks over to Bray and hands him the bottle of meds. "One pill every four hours for the next three days, not to exceed six pills in a twenty-four hour period. I suppose you could skip the nightly treatment by giving her two at bedtime if you wish. Make sure she has plenty of food and water if you want her to heal quickly." The doctor pauses and then looks from one shifter to the other. "Or don't, I suppose. If you want her in pain longer, then do whatever you please, but if you aren't going to use those meds, bring them back. My stock is running low."

When he leaves the room, Fausto gives the doctor's receding figure the middle finger and mumbles *motherfucker* under his breath.

Bray fumbles with the lid on the bottle and pulls out a single pill. "Do you need water or can you dry swallow?"

I'd do anything for some pain relief right now. The pill could be five times the size and I'd chew it if I had to. "I can dry swallow it."

When I first met Bray, he seemed like the most dangerous of the three. He bared his teeth at me and the inflamed look in his eyes made me fear for my life. But it seems like underneath all that bravado is a gentleman.

He helps me to my feet when Levar returns with a t-shirt and a pair of shorts. Bray helps me out of my vomit-stained sweatpants and into the soft, satin shorts provided by the doctor. He lets me lean on him as I step into the pants and then he makes sure they're comfortable on my waist. Putting on my shirt is a task that results in multiple gasps of pain before it's situated appropriately on my body.

Levar places my arm in a sling and tells me to be careful. "Don't put any weight on it. Don't perform any magic with it."

"I don't have any magic," I reply tonelessly.

He doesn't skip a beat. "Good, then there will be no further risk of injury. In three days when your cycle of meds is finished, you should try moving your arm around a little bit every day until you have a full range of motion back. It will take a few weeks, maybe a month, but there doesn't seem to be any permanent damage."

He rounds on Fausto and looks up at him blandly. "I'd like to see her again in a week to make sure she's doing alright, but if that's inconvenient due to her *status*...," he trails off.

Fausto rolls his eyes at the doctor. "I'll bring her back in a week," he answers sarcastically. "C'mon, Bray. Let's get her back downstairs."

I wish I'd gotten to spend a few minutes alone with the doctor; I might have been able to convince him to set me free. But since I didn't, I guess it's time to return to my cell. Just another night with Rigo and Bilia, my new best friends.

FAUSTO

I'm such an idiot. I dislocated the girl's shoulder and now Bray gets to be the hero. It makes me burn with rage when an alarm goes off every four hours indicating that it's time for him to check on Elspeth and give her the pain meds Levar prescribed. I hate Bray. And I hate that stupid fucking doctor.

Levar's been around for decades. He helped the last three packs of Kings before us. He patched up their wounded and cured their sickness before it spread through the Forbidden Lands. He came with recommendations from men and women all throughout the Forbidden Lands. That didn't make him any less insufferable.

"What's got your panties in a twist?" Arcturus asks as we patrol the streets. He's poised to transition at any moment and flexes his fingers at his sides. For the largest wolf in all of the Forbidden Lands, he's also the most paranoid. He's been convinced ever since he took the throne that someone will try to catch him off guard in an attempt to take it from him.

"You look insecure as fuck right now," I grumble at him. I avert my eyes before he can see jealousy raging inside of them.

Once crudely made, our Main Street has gotten an incredible makeover since we took control of the crown and the Forbidden Lands. I singlehandedly helped rebuild 90% of the buildings that housed our retail sector. I have the scars, aches, and pains to prove it. I usually enjoy patrol because I get a chance to check out my handiwork, but today it makes me morose.

Arcturus snorts before leaving me to check out the inn; I have no choice but to follow him. He's already leaning up against the bar flirting with the owner. "Holi, come on," he says with a pout, "just a couple of pints for Fausto and me. We won't be long."

The smile on her face is thin, but it's the blush on her cheeks that tells me she's flattered by his attention. "Oh, alright, but don't be long," Holi warns, repeating his words back to him. She waggles her finger before turning to grab his requested pints from the shelf. "Like I said, I need to close up early." It takes her all of twenty seconds to fill the pints and slide them across the counter toward Arcturus.

He reaches into his pocket and pulls out a handful of coins, sliding them across the wood. "Feel free to close down around us. We're just going to have a drink and then leave. We appreciate you serving us."

Despite the pushback Arcturus received for being so young when he challenged the former first point of the crown, he had the charisma to win most of the packs over when he won his fight. A smile here, a compliment there, he knew just what to say and when. It made me sick. Or maybe it just made me jealous.

"Tell me what's up," Arcturus ushers me toward a table.

I take a seat across from him and ask about Holi. "What's she closing up early for, anyway?"

Arcturus shrugs his shoulders before taking a generous swig of ale. "Her daughter is going through her first heat. Nothing to worry yourself about. Now tell me why you spent the whole patrol scowling at everyone we passed. Frankly, you're pissing the packs off more than usual."

"It wasn't intentional," I grumble. I allow myself a drink and when the ale goes down easy, so do all my frustrations. I breathe out a sigh of anger and lay my problems on Arcturus. "I didn't mean to dislocate her shoulder, you know?"

"Ah," he nods his head wisely, "so it *is* about Elspeth. Are you jealous that Bray is spending all that time with her? You think she'll like him better?" He taunts.

It shouldn't bother me who she likes or doesn't like. She belongs to the three of us regardless of her preferences. If I demand that she come to my bed, she can't deny me on the basis of liking Bray more. "This is taking too long," I glare at the table. "I thought this process of making her our queen would be moving along faster." Even I can hear the whine in my tone and I hate myself for it.

Arcturus purses his lips and then takes another swill of his drink. He makes a sound of relief when he slams the pint back on the table. "She's a girl, Fausto, a girl that was purposefully suppressed all her life. This isn't what we thought we were getting, but that just means it might take a few more weeks to come to fruition. She needs us to lead her to her awakening as a shifter and sexually," he adds with a provocative waggle of his brows.

I raise my eyes from the wood to look at him. "What?" I question sharply.

"That girl is a virgin," Arcturus says with a smirk, "I can smell her unpopped cherry every time I get close to her. You can't?"

He asks in a condescending sort of way and I flip him the bird. "Fuck you, Arc." He snorts again before burying his face in the last of the ale. "Who gets to," I pause as I search for the right words, "*deflower* her?" We have to be appropriate in this very public setting, especially when Holi is wiping down the bar with an ear tuned to our conversation.

The two of us stare at one another and I can feel a line being drawn in the sand. Arcturus knows I asked the question in hopes it would be me. I know that he expects Bray and me to allow it to be him. "Maybe we should leave that up to her," he finally says after a tense few moments, his words meant to put me at ease.

My cock tightens the front of my pants just thinking about it. It's been a while since I last broke a woman's seal. She screamed for a few seconds as my thick, engorged shaft tore her open. Specks of her blood stained my member when I pulled out of her. In between, she yelled my name while digging her nails into my back.

The memory is so evocative that I tighten my hand around the glass and pray that it doesn't break. To salve my new arousal, I chug half the pint of ale. "Maybe we should push the issue," I announce as I set the glass down a little harder than I intended. "Get her to share her flower with all of us. Maybe it'll quicken her awakening when the beast inside of her is released." God, I'm a selfish man. And a sexual one. I want to feel her tight little body beneath me as I bury myself inside of her.

A smirk tugs the corner of Arcturus' lip upward. "You might be onto something, Fausto."

Relief floods through my veins; I don't know what I would have done if he'd said no.

ELSPETH

Every four hours for three days, excluding nights, Bray showed up. He brought a cup of water and a pill with him. The guard opened the cell door and he'd come inside and sit with me for a while. To say that Rigo and Bilia were upset would be an understatement.

The first time it happened, Bilia screamed bloody murder for five minutes straight. After that, Bray couldn't take it anymore and he had her removed from the cell. Rigo sat with his back against the wall, arms crossed over his chest, eyeing the both of us with deep suspicion.

Bray never hurt me though. He asked me how I was doing and if my shoulder was starting to feel better. Courtesy of the pills provided by the doctor, I hadn't felt pain since taking my first in his office. But they made me really sleepy and I sheepishly admitted to Bray that I slept through dinner that first night.

"They didn't leave it for you?" He asked with a frown. "To eat when you woke up?"

I wondered if he'd been a prisoner in his own cells before, or if he had any say in what happened down here at all. "This isn't a hotel," I told him gently. "I was lucky to get that first set of clothes before I saw you guys again."

I must have said the wrong thing. An hour after Bray left, the guard was standing at the front of my cell snarling. "You little bitch. You ratted me out to the Kings." He opened the cell door and stormed in, pushing his disfigured, ugly face into mine. Spittle coated my cheeks when he roared in my face, "Do it again, bitch. Watch what happens then."

Bray asked about the guard during our next meeting. "I warned him that if he delayed following through with an order from me again, it would be his last. Did he give you any trouble?"

Rigo had urged me to tell Bray about the mistreatment, especially because the guard shoved me backward and slammed my head into the wall. For an hour the entire world was spinning and my skull throbbed harder than my dislocated shoulder. But I didn't want to see anyone else behind these bars with me, not even the surly guard keeping an eye on us day and night. "No, no trouble," I lied.

By the third day, Bilia was used to Bray's presence. She'd admitted to me the night before that the reason she was here was because she'd tried to kill Bray when he was in post-coital bliss. It made her earlier pronouncements that Bray was 'mad, mad, mad' that much easier to understand. Not that she told me why she tried to kill him. I think if she had, it might have given me a different perspective of him.

Rigo distrusted Bray. Every time he left, Rigo would launch himself at the bars and tell me that I needed to end this. "He's using you. He wants something from you. He is not that nice."

It was all true, but I couldn't stop Bray any more than Rigo could. Every day I watched my prison mate leave his cell and be escorted upstairs. He'd return an hour later with a solemn look on his face and a glare ready-made for me. Unlike that first day, he didn't come back with a bloody foot, but he did come back with new bandages.

"What do they do to you?" I asked him once.

Rigo shook his head and laid down on his cot. He didn't feel the need to explain himself to me. I never found out what they did to him upstairs.

"This isn't very comfortable," Bray announced once when he arrived during lunch. He took a seat on my bed and his nose wrinkled in disgust as he tried to relax.

I scarfed down a sandwich that had cold meat this

time. It tasted a bit like leather, but food was food. "I didn't realize you wanted us to be comfortable."

Bray looked through the bars of my cell and sneered when he met Rigo's gaze. "I don't want everyone to be comfortable," he said, "just you." The latter part he said more quietly.

I didn't dare tell him that if that was the case, they could move me somewhere else. Somewhere with a mattress that hadn't been flatted by a thousand bodies before mine. Somewhere the meat was hot and tasted like chicken or beef. Somewhere the water ran free and the toilets didn't.

"What is that?" Bray asked when he finally turned back to look at me and the tray I'd been given. "Is that what we're serving you?"

The day's vegetables had been pureed. Its orange texture made me think that it might be some kind of squash. The bread was hard, but the cheese was alright. "Yes?" I responded, unsure of what he was asking.

Bray grabbed my spoon and dipped it in the tiniest bit of pureed vegetable. When he brought it to his lips, it barely touched his tongue before he was spitting it out on the floor. "What is this?!" He yelled as he grabbed my cup of water and used it to wash his mouth out. "That's disgusting."

"That was my only water until dinner." My jaw dropped. I still wasn't drinking the morning milk we were offered and now he'd drank my only water since dinner the night before. He arrived earlier with a pill and some water, but it was barely more than a swig. "I haven't had anything to drink since yesterday."

It took Bray a few seconds to realize that he was holding my water cup. He looked at it and then back at me. "What?" His eyes looked feral as he questioned me.

I set my sandwich down on the tray and explained to him the daily meals. I told him about the milk that I couldn't drink with breakfast because of my lactose issues. I told him that there were no drinks in between meals, which meant you either drank from your toilet or waited for the next meal to arrive. And believe me, the toilet water was questionable at best.

"No," Bray mumbled to himself several times, "this isn't right."

I had hardened during my week in the prison cell. I was growing accustomed to sixteen ounces of water being my only source of hydration for the day. "This is a prison, Bray. I don't know what you expect. It's *your* prison, no less. It's not like you have to treat prisoners fairly when you're going to kill them anyway."

My tone offended him. Bray got up and left. The guard returned a few minutes later with a larger cup full of water and grumbled under his breath as he set it outside of my cell. "Stupid girl with her stupid special perks."

I savored every ounce of water that Bray had sent. It wasn't much, but it brought color back to my cheeks.

During the three days that I was receiving daily meds, the Mad Kings never summoned me to the throne room. I assumed it was because Bray could keep an eye on me during his regular visits. But the evening of the fourth day, after the visits had stopped and my special perk of talking to someone other than Rigo or Bilia had ended, the guard returned with a leer. "The Kings want ya," he said with a shit-eating grin on his face. "Maybe you'll come back in a cast this time."

He led me up the stairs and handed me off at the top. This time I wasn't taken to the throne room. This time I was taken to a grand room with ornate carvings on the door. "Good luck," the guard commented as he twisted open the doors.

ELSPETH

They sit around a table clad in loose, white shirts and black, tight-fitting pants. Before them is a meal fit for kings. My mouth waters.

"Come in," Arcturus gestures me over. "We were waiting for you."

My stomach twists in knots as I take slow steps toward the trio. Fausto's blonde mane has been brushed. The dip of Bray's shirt shows off a few sparse curls of hair on his chest. Arcturus looks positively handsome with his beaming smile and kind eyes. These are not the men who threatened me four days ago.

"We'd like you to have dinner with us," Fausto raises a glass of amber liquid. There is a layer of foam

on the top that I only notice when he gives me an air
cheers. "Bray told us about the conditions of the prison.
While many of the individuals down there deserve the
treatment they're receiving, you are our Queen. You
deserve the finest foods."

I can barely look at him or the other two Kings. At
the mention of food, I find my eyes feasting on grilled
fish and freshly made mashed potatoes. Vegetables
swim in a lake of butter, the smell of which is divine.
The twisting in my stomach changes to growling. It
feels like an eternity since I last had a good meal.

"You deserve to be hand fed." Arcturus grabs a
grape from his plate and rises from his chair. As he
approaches me, I shift my eyes from the delicacies on
the table to his smiling face. "You should see what
exists beyond the edge of your world. Open up."

My heart is pounding in my chest. I dare to part
my lips and feel the cool skin of the grape pass
between them. "Bite," he whispers a second later.
Arcturus withdraws his fingers slowly, swiping his
thumb across my bottom lip.

I bite into the proffered grape and heaven spurts
from the fruit. It's unlike any grape I've ever tasted
before, or perhaps that's the hunger talking.

"We have fields that span for a hundred miles,"
Arcturus answers my unasked question. "Men and
women tend the fields to provide for all the packs in
the Forbidden Lands. We don't have to worry about

silly things like money or fashion or politics. We worry about taking care of one another. We are a community."

The residue of the grape remains on my tongue long after I've swallowed it. Like the greedy woman I am, I want more. I want to taste everything on the table.

"Join us for dinner. Enjoy the fruits of our labor. And the vegetables. And the meats," he adds with a smile. "This is what every meal will be like, Elspeth. Endless stores of wine and ale. Every delectable treat that you can fathom." Arcturus turns to face the table. "Meals that will actually, truly fill you." He walks away, returns to his seat, and makes himself comfortable. "You will join us, won't you?"

I enthusiastically nod my head yes. There is nothing more that I want than to scarf down everything in front of me. A dark pie sits in the center of the table and the sweet smell of blueberries calls to me like a siren to a sailor. "Yes, of course."

I walk forward to take my seat and find that there is none. The table is large and round, weighted down with food and beverages. But despite all the space, there are only three place settings. "I-I, there's no chair," I frown.

Bray casually pats his lap in response. "That's not true. I have a chair for you right here."

My throat feels like the desert and I try to swallow

saliva to wet my arid vocal cords.

"Or you could sit in my chair." Fausto pats his lap as well, ushering me forward to take a seat. "The roasted duck is amazing. It's moist, tender, and just a little fatty. Once you have a taste, you'll be licking my fingertips begging for more."

Arcturus just places his hand on his thigh and looks at me with a carefree grin. "Take any seat, Elspeth, and we can chat about the first thing that comes up."

I have a feeling that he doesn't mean my thoughts on the standard of care his prisoners receive and the state of his dungeons. "I-I'm not sure I'm that hungry." My stomach roars in protest, loud enough to cut through the silence and alert the men to my lie.

"Now, Elspeth," Fausto frowns, "it isn't nice to lie to the men you will marry. That kind of behavior is unacceptable."

Men. I. Will. Marry. All three of them, my future husbands. I grasp for words but none come to me. My mind is devoid of thought and my brain can't function enough to form a sentence.

"Elspeth," Arcturus' tone turns darker, "pick a seat. Now. You won't like what happens if you don't."

My arm is still in a sling from the last time I saw the three of them together. The memory of the pain they inflicted on me is still burned into my brain. If the guard has his way, I'll go back to my prison cell in a cast. And frankly, I wouldn't put it past the Mad Kings to make his fucked up wish come true.

You're getting a real *dinner*, the little voice in my head says. *Suck it up and eat as much as you can. Eat until you're sick if you have to. This might be the only real food you get for the rest of your life.* If I don't come around to their way of thinking, the little voice could be right. I'll die without tasting roasted duck or burying my problems in blueberry pie. *It's only one night. You can handle whatever they do to you.*

I take a tentative step toward Fausto. He sits only a few feet away and offers me a charming smile. It is a deep contrast from the man who earlier looked like he might kill me if I didn't agree that my grandmother is Alize Nikae.

When I am only a few inches away, I meet his gaze with my simple, unassuming one. What do I do now? Just climb onto his lap?

He answers me as if he can read my thoughts. "Ask me politely if you can take a seat."

I swallow the lump forming in my throat. "Can I sit here?" The words are spoken meekly, making my stomach turn as I realize he's making me beg to sit in his lap.

Fausto rubs a spot on his thigh as he pushes his

chair back a few inches. "By all means. It'll be my pleasure. Maybe yours, too."

I'm terrified for my life, but I turn around and seat
myself on his strong, thick thighs. I can feel something
pressing into my backside, but I try to ignore it.
"Thank you," is all that I can choke out as Fausto leans
up against me from behind.

He grabs the carving knife in front of me and a
fork, wrapping his arms around my body as he looks
over my shoulder to see what he's doing. "Let me get
you a slice of the duck," Fausto insists.

Across the table, Bray is watching with dark desire
clouding his gaze. Arcturus scoops himself a plate of
food while staring in our direction. They can't help
themselves. There is a show premiering over here and
they have front-row seats.

Fausto places a portion of the roasted duck on the
plate in front of me, then goes to work cutting it into
small, bite-sized portions. When he sets the carving
knife back down on the table, it's well within my
reach.

For one fleeting moment, I consider grabbing it
and stabbing him. I would still have to get through
Bray and Arcturus before I got out of the room, and
then I'd probably have to take care of the guard, but if I
could stomach four murders, I might make it back to
the Cersei district.

But it doesn't matter. Fausto grabs a piece of the roasted duck between his fingers and brings it to my lips. "Taste," he commands. And all my thoughts of stabbing and escape are washed away by the scent of the savory fowl before me.

He's barely popped the bird between my lips when I feel his other hand reach between my legs. Shame spreads across my face as I chew the meat. "Shh," he whispers in my ear, "don't make a sound."

His fingers dash across the front of my shorts. It feels like an electric shock as he caresses such a sensitive part of me. While he's grabbing the next bite of roasted duck with one hand, he's rubbing my clit with his other.

I am embarrassed by the way I squirm in his lap, shifting from one side to the other. I don't know if I'm trying to maneuver his fingers to touch me the right way or if I'm trying to escape his touches completely. It almost doesn't matter. The more that he feeds me, the more rigorous his fingers become. I can barely chew the bite in my mouth when I'm panting with need.

"Isn't it tender?" Fausto asks as he fingers another piece. I am silently begging that he stop. Stop the feeding, stop the touching, stop everything so that I can come to my senses. "Isn't it *moist*?"

Does he know what's going on between my

thighs? That I am dripping with arousal from the way he plays with me? His cock is rigid under me, now fully extended and taking the brunt of my squirms. Every time I shift in one direction, I feel the press of his member against my core and it makes me want to explode.

"This could all be yours," he whispers once more. "The food, the pleasure, the attention of every man in the room."

Bray and Arcturus aren't even pretending to eat anymore. They watch with smoldering eyes as I dance in my seat, bringing myself closer and closer to orgasm with every passing moment. The pretense of dinner is forgotten when Fausto's fingers tap just the right notes on my clit through my shorts.

I toss my head back, arching my back with frustration as I wait for the release to come. "Stop," I beg. I don't want it to be like this. I don't want every eye in the room staring at me when I orgasm.

"You want it," Fausto growls in my ear. "Tell me you want it and I'll let you come."

I am feeble beneath his ministrations; he's right. I whimper and try to close my legs to him, but that doesn't stop his fingers from moving against me. "Okay, I want it," I announce as I lean into him. "I want it. Please. I want it."

This is a different kind of torture than the prisoners in the dungeon have gone through before. My body has not been marred nor my psyche destroyed. Instead, I am fraught with pleasure and the shameful realization that this is just as effective as pain. My body craves to be touched now and it weakens my resolve.

ARCTURUS

The touch of desperation in her voice as she tells Fausto she wants it is an endorphin rush. I watch as her teeth press into his bottom lip, staining the pale pink skin a dark red from the blood rush. I see her body contort and writhe on my best friend's lap as she fully embraces her orgasm. Her eyes close and the moans that escape between her lips sound like the sweetest song.

Bray openly strokes himself a few feet away. He pushed out his chair to give himself more room to drag his hand up and down his shaft as he stares at the entertainment on the other side of the table. "I want her," he growls when she leans into Fausto and rests her head against his shoulder. The pleasure from her orgasm recedes like a wave, wiping her body of energy. But she is weakened, not deaf.

Elspeth's eyes pop open and her lips part in protest. Then she sees the scene playing out before her. Bray is firmly tugging himself, his hand racing along his member as he looks at her with dark, lust-filled eyes. "I-I-I," she starts to stutter.

"You would look exquisite bouncing up and down on my cock," he whispers across the expanse. "Take a little seat right here," he pats his thigh aggressively. "Put your hands on the table and ride me, gorgeous."

Pink colors her cheeks and I don't know if she's frightened or embarrassed. Her mouth opens and closes like a fish gasping for air.

"Put it away," I order Bray.

He pins me with a sharp look. If we were in our shifted forms, I think he would have nipped at me. "So Fausto gets to have fun but not me." If it's a question, it sure doesn't sound like one; Bray says it like he's accusing me of betraying him. "I spent three days making sure she was okay after that buffoon," he shoves his finger in Fausto's direction, "dislocated her shoulder. I deserve to touch her body more than he does."

I'd give anything to be cock-deep inside of Elspeth right now. To feel her virgin pussy tighten around me as I sink into her depths. But she looks unprepared for that. The fear radiating off her skin gives the air a sickeningly sweet tinge. If I were to take her or let Bray have his way with her, we would risk breaking her beyond repair. "Elspeth, please, take a plate and grab what you'd like. You may take it to your cell."

She works her way off Fausto's lap, her eyes trained on the ground as she moves. She looks around for a plate before taking Fausto's and gathering up some food from the table. When she scurries away, she mumbles a *thank you* as she passes me.

"What the fuck, Arc?" Bray roars as the door opens and she slips through the crack. "I thought tonight was the night."

Half the food on the table that's supposed to be hot has now cooled. Regardless, I grab some mashed potatoes and pour gravy atop them. "This isn't just any girl, Bray. If I let you have her and she didn't want it, she would have been scarred for life."

Bray stands up and slams his down on the table. "She wanted it. Or weren't you paying attention? I heard her begging for it from that fucker," he glares across the table at Fausto.

"Me?" Fausto brings the fingers up to his nose that he just used to get Elspeth off. "You should smell her. She is heavenly."

It's up to me to break up the fight that starts. Bray doesn't need to be in his wolf form to lose his shit on someone. He throws himself across the table at Fausto and a cacophony of shouts is quick to follow. "You piece of shit. You think you deserve her after what you did?"

I know I should stop the fight. A little voice in my head urges me to get up and tell the two of them to knock it off. But the sound of flesh hitting flesh provides a different sort of dinner entertainment.

"Oh, and you think bringing her some meds earns you the right to stick your dick in her?" Fausto's nose is bleeding, but either he doesn't know or he doesn't care. He continues to block blows from Bray who's sitting on top of him and lashing out like a feral animal. Every thwarted hit is followed by Fausto's laughter.

"More so than you, sick fuck."

Bray's a loose cannon. It's one of the reasons we've been in the newspapers around Meira'mor. Though we plan our attacks on the districts thoroughly and execute them only when we're sure nothing will go wrong, something always goes wrong and it's usually Bray who's there when it happens. God forbid he takes it on the chin like a normal person though. Instead, he starts fights we didn't come for or attacks people we never meant to hurt.

Before he can get in too much damage, I reluctantly get up and separate the two of them. Bray looks like he's about to foam at the mouth and Fausto is taunting him from the ground. I give the latter a kick in the leg and tell him to shut up. "This isn't about fucking that girl and getting our rocks off, so both of you quit it."

I shove Bray away from me, daring him to raise his fists at me next. So help me God, I'll knock him the fuck out if I have to.

"I thought breeding her was half the fun, Arc," Bray taunts instead. A bruise is already blooming on his cheekbone, the body's traumatic response to taking a crack from Fausto when they were rolling around.

"It is." I can't help but shake my head in frustration at him. "But that's not the only thing she's good for. We need her to be the queen. We need her to lead our packs into battle and unite the community. She can't do that if she's crying in her prison cell because someone got a little too handsy too fast. We don't have to wine and dine her, but Christ, we have to make sure she wants it." Before Bray can open his mouth and tell me again that she was begging for it, I cut him off with a point of my finger. "And if you'd have seen the same look in her eyes that I did, you would have realized that she *didn't* want it. Not like this. She needs more time."

Bray's strength grows when he's angry. He grabs the edge of the table and flips it upside down. Food goes flying everywhere, including on the three of us. "I'm tired of waiting, Arc. That girl is ours. She's our property. If she doesn't start returning dividends on our investment, I might just take them from her."

As he storms off, Fausto leisurely gets to his feet.

He touches his face and his fingers come back bloody. "Shit," he mumbles.

If he shifts, he'll be healed in no time. "Go do some patrols or something," I order. "Clean yourself up."

"He's right, you know," Fausto rights the table, but it doesn't help the mess. "We deserve the product we paid for. We've been too lenient."

I raise a hand to cut him off; I don't want to hear it anymore. "I'll handle it, Fausto." And I will. I won't fuck an unwilling girl, but there are other ways to break Elspeth the way she needs to be broken. I'll make her pliable to our mission even if it causes more initial harm than good.

And thankfully, there's more than one way to skin a cat.

ELSPETH

Two nights ago I was licking the floors of my prison cell trying to get up every last drop of food the guard had casually tossed on the ground. He took my plate from the dining room away from me, but not before emptying its contents. "You want it so bad, eat it now." He crushed a berry with the toe of his shoe, but that didn't stop me. Hunger drives a person to do crazy things.

Now, after two days of silence, I sit in my cell and watch the sun slowly peek through the grimy bit of window just out of Bilia's reach. She was taken to the throne room yesterday, or wherever it is the Mad Kings take the prisoners. She returned with a spring in her step despite the bruises blossoming on her face and torso. "I can take a little beating," she explained, "the real torture is what happens in the room at the top of the stairs."

I couldn't recall seeing a room at the top of the stairs, but I'd only been taken up the stairs a few times. Instead of looking for torture rooms, I'd been looking for a way out.

Bilia woke up an hour ago and started stretching. Usually a quiet task, she somehow managed to make enough noise to wake both Rigo and me. She didn't apologize.

Now she was lying on her cot snoring while Rigo read his book and I watched the sun filter through the window. We live a charmed existence, I'm sure. I remember never having free time back home. I was always flitting from one room to the next or one district to another, learning new skills or offering my services to people in need. I didn't have time to breathe, ponder the mysteries of the universe, or even take a nap.

I had all the time in the world to do that now and I can't remember what I missed so much. Pondering the mysteries of the universe is nice until you realize that your universe has shrunk dramatically and your world now consists of three men who put you on edge while simultaneously doing nice things for you. The contrast between the two is the land where I lay my spinning head.

"We should wake her up," Rigo says after a while.

Bilia's snoring drives him crazy. He has banged on the cement wall between their two cells on more than one occasion. "It would only be fair after her earlier shenanigans."

I agree with him, but it's also the loneliness talking. When Bilia is awake, I can chat with both of them for hours. I've learned a lot about my prison friends, including where they're from and why they're here. But out of respect for our newly formed friendship, I shrug my shoulders and tell Rigo that waking Bilia up isn't going to solve our problems.

Frankly, I don't know what, if anything, *would* solve our problems. Rigo is here for starting a conspiracy to dethrone the Mad Kings. He was in the process of gathering packs together to force the Kings' hand when he was arrested. He doesn't expect to smell fresh air ever again. His fate is tied to however long the Kings let him live.

I can almost relate to his struggle. I didn't want to dethrone anyone, sure, but my fate is also tied to what the Kings want. At any moment they could request my presence and decide that I'm not worth the trouble anymore.

That's the thought that haunts me in the dead of night. When the darkness enshrouds the windows and the overhead lights are dimmed, I hide beneath my blankets and cry. That's the only place that feels safe anymore. It's the only time people aren't staring or leering at me, asking me questions, or demanding that I do magic I've never performed before. My blankets have become a safe haven, even if they are smelly and scratchy.

"I think they're coming for you today." Rigo has been taken to visit the Kings every day since my arrival. He won't tell me what it's about, but I have a feeling that it's about me. I can tell from the way he shoots me confused and angry looks like he can't tell whether he's upset with me or if he feels sorry for me.

I shrug my shoulders even though Rigo isn't looking this way. "They have to come back for me eventually," I sigh.

It's the spine of his book cracking back into place that draws my attention. From across the prison, I see his blue eyes looking my way. "Tell me why, Elspeth. What do they want from you? We've told you who we are and what we've done."

Isn't it enough that I give him my milk every morning? That on the night I returned from dinner, I tossed a few uncrushed berries his way? Why does he need to know so much?

"What does telling me change?" Rigo asks, changing tact. "You're still going to be in that cell. We're still going to be across from you. The Kings are still going to torture all of us. Just tell me."

He has a point. If I tell him or not, the world is still

going to keep spinning. "Have you ever heard of Alize Nikae?"

Realization registers on Rigo's face for only a second before he forces his features back into passivity. "Yes," he pauses, "Well, I know what I learned in school, which is that she was kidnapped a few decades ago or something. The Nikae women were like, in charge of the Forbidden Lands or something. Or maybe they found the Forbidden Lands. I don't remember."

So this *is* common knowledge. It isn't something we're taught in Meira'mor, but we also aren't taught about the Forbidden Lands, either. The map of Meira'mor ends after the Cersei district. The land beyond isn't talked about. The only reason we're informed about what exists is because we're one of the biggest districts that the shifters pillage.

"The Kings believe, incorrectly so," I close my eyes and shake my head in indignation that I have to spread this lie, "that I'm Alize Nikae's granddaughter."

Rigo releases a gasp that I'm sure half the prison heard. It's loud enough to wake Bilia.

"Wha?" She raises her head. "What's going on?"

Rigo drops the book in his lap on the floor when he stands and races to the bars. He presses his face into the small space between the metal with his eyes widening in curiosity. "You are the forgotten queen?"

For the love of Christ. Not this again. "I knew I

shouldn't have told you. Should have taken that secret to the grave. That's my fault."

"You don't know what this means, Elspeth. You're royalty. This explains so much," he starts to mumble. I catch words like *blankets, food,* and *Bray* between other muffled announcements.

It makes me groan in despair. I always open my mouth and shove my foot right inside. "I'm not even related to her, Rigo. I'm not a shifter or anything. I barely have any magic at all."

This stops his rant right in its tracks. He started pacing his cell, but now he stops and looks at me. "That's why you don't have a collar." Rigo brings his hand up to the metal around his neck and fingers the collar until his skin catches on a snag and rips open. He brings his bleeding digit to his mouth, sucking on it until the blood is gone. "The Kings wouldn't have you if they weren't sure," he keeps muttering to himself. "What does this all mean?"

Nothing, I want to tell him. It means nothing. It means that they kidnapped the wrong girl and now I'm being forced to live out a fantasy I never wanted. There's another girl out there that's supposed to be locked up in this cell trying to come to terms with her future. It isn't supposed to be me.

The loud footsteps of the guard interrupt Rigo before he can do more digging. "The Kings want to see you," he says gruffly.

This guard is new; I've never seen him before. He's short and squat, but he carries a baton and a set of keys that jingle when he manually unlocks the door to my cell. "C'mon, girl. We don't have much time." He's gentler than the other guard and he doesn't even grab me when I walk out of the cell.

What happened to the last guy?

ELSPETH

When I open my eyes, I'm shrouded in
darkness. My body aches and I feel light-
headed. The room is spinning and I can't
even see it. Everything feels like it's just slightly
off-kilter and vibrating. Oh god, the vibrating.

I try to sit up and find that my wrists and forearms
are strapped to the bed. No matter, the searing pain
that shoots through my torso when I move is enough
to deter me from trying again. I lie there with my teeth
gritted and try to remember what happened.

Good of you to join us, Elspeth. Arcturus wore a
cruel smile along with a shirt whose neckline
plummeted so drastically that I could almost see his
belly button. I remember thinking in a fleeting sort

of way that his smile made my stomach feel warm despite the apprehension rising within me like a tide.

Bray was standing beside Arcturus, twirling a knife deftly between his fingers. I couldn't help but think that it was dangerous, that at any second the knife could slip and cut through skin and tendons.

Fausto was nowhere to be found. Until he was.

He crept up behind me, I think. After the doors were closed and I approached Arcturus and Bray, he must have come out of hiding. I remember surprise ringing through me when his arms wrapped around mine and pulled them behind my back. "You were breathtaking when you were moaning with pleasure. It made us wonder how ravishing you'd look when you're screaming in pain."

I'm jolted back to reality when a door opens and light filters into the room. I feel the presence of bodies all around me and close my eyes out of fear. If they don't know I'm awake, I don't have to talk to them. Whoever *they* are.

"She's been in and out of consciousness for a few hours," says a familiar voice. "She lost a lot of blood, but we think the transfusions have helped."

I recognize Fausto's voice immediately. "Arc and Bray are in their rooms recovering. I know some of this

is our fault, but we didn't mean for this to happen."
The apology sounds half-hearted.

I think the other person is the doctor, Levar. He
pulls back the blanket covering my chest and I feel a
rush of cool air across my body. "I don't know what
you guys are up to, but you tell me if those marks are
worth it."

Fingers press softly against a bandage on my chest,
just over my heart. "It's difficult to explain," Fausto
trails off.

"You don't have to explain it to me, Fausto." The
doctor replaces the blanket, covering me once more.
"But half the floor is littered with bodies. What did the
mainlanders want? Why would they attack us in our
own home?"

My eyes pop open and I go to sit up again, stopped
by the shackles and the pain. "The mainlanders? Was
it my dad? Did my father come for me?"

I catch Fausto and Levar off guard. Fausto's eyes
harden while the doctor soothes me with comforting
words. "Please, don't move too much," he sits on the
bed beside me and readjusts the blanket. "You'll start
bleeding through your bandages again."

Fausto reaches out to press the back of his hand to
my forehead. "She's sweating. She's got to be running
a fever," he says to Levar. "Her forehead is burning up."

Levar gets up and walks over to the medicine
cabinet I saw the last time I was in the room. He turns

on a light that makes my eyes sting. "Her body is trying to fight off the infection." He returns a few moments later with a couple of leaves. "Place these under your tongue to soften them, then chew and swallow."

I look at the proffered plant with a glare. "No. What is that?

Levar sighs impatiently. "Soursop."

I've used soursop before, but as a way to keep patients asleep during minor procedures. "I don't want that. I don't want to sleep anymore. I want to know what happened."

The doctor gives Fausto a hard look as if to say *this is your mess,* you *clean it up.* But Fausto pinches the bridge of his nose looking frustrated.

"I know what you did to me," I accuse with a glare. "I know that you branded me like an animal. I remember."

Fausto held my arms behind me as Arcturus took Bray's knife and made the first incision. He ripped the sleeve of my tank top down, unveiling the flesh above my left breast. "I'd say that this is going to hurt me more than it's going to hurt you, but I'd be lying." Arcturus flashed me a grin before digging the knife into my skin.

. . .

My throat is hoarse from screaming. I didn't notice it before, but now I feel tendrils of pain from my earlier screams.

"Do you remember the attack then?" Fausto returns my glare. "Do you remember Bray trying to protect you when your father's stupid little minions tried to kill you?"

My father's soldiers would never do that; they've spent their entire lives trying to keep me safe. "You're lying," but the words sound unsure even to my own ears.

Fausto snorts in derision. "We might be responsible for the initials carved into your shoulder, but we aren't responsible for this." He grabs the blanket and rips it back, ignoring Levar's protests.

I lift my head and see bandages covering my torso. They drug their knife across my shoulder, but the large swathes of hospital dressings cover my right side from rib to hip.

"One of his men used his teeth to try and pry you out of Bray's grip. You're lucky you only need one kidney because you lost the other one." Fausto is shaking his head at me as if this is my fault. "Bray nearly died. He could barely shift by the time the raid was finished. It'll take him days to heal."

I don't know why Fausto is so mad. "Why are you blaming me?"

Fausto turns and grabs the first thing in sight. The glass shatters when he throws it with all his force at the wall. "We put our lives on the line for you and you still called for your father after Arcturus had run them off. We saved you from being torn apart *at the behest of your father* and you still preferred him to us. I'm not angry about the raid; we knew it would come eventually, but we listened to your father tell his men to kill you over leaving here without you, and you *still* hail him as your hero. That man is poison, Elspeth, and you are too happy to drink from the vial."

Levar steps between Fausto and me. The only one of the Mad Kings still standing is practically foaming at the mouth. "Go," the doctor orders, his tone leaving no room for argument. "There will be plenty of time to discuss this when she's healed. Go check on Bray."

Fausto steps up to the doctor like he might put a fist through his face, but the toxic silence is broken with a roar. He spins on his heel and slams his fist into the wall. It's followed by the sickening sound of bones crunching as they come in contact with stone.

"Take these. Now." Levar turns and shoves the leaves at me again. "You will not heal if you do not rest. You and the other injured non-shifters on the floor are my priority, *not* him."

I open my mouth and let Levar put the leaves beneath my tongue. He busies himself with checking my bandages while I wait for the medicine to take effect. Lurking in the corner of my mind is a memory that I buried.

I saw my father's eyes in the throne room, more menacing than he'd ever been before. He tried to kill the guard at the door while his soldiers filed in one after the other to take out the Mad Kings.

I don't remember him saying that he'd rather see me dead than in the Kings' grasp, but it almost makes sense. The soldier that tried to save me didn't have to dig his teeth into my stomach. He didn't have to break my ribs and destroy my kidney beyond repair.

But the memory drifts away as sleep pulls me under. Goodbye, hard truths, I'll see you on the other side.

BRAY

The golden halo of the sun in my room slowly starts to disappear. Little by little, it inches down the floor. It is replaced by moonlight beaming through the window. Where the gold once stood, now there is a halo of white.

Chunks of my life pass in darkness. I try to make myself comfortable on the bed, but I'm too weak to move into the position I want to be in, which is stretched out and under five layers of blankets. I fall asleep freezing only to wake up sweating, no longer wanting to be under any blankets at all.

Fausto comes around when the sun is up and again when the moon is high in the sky. He shifts into his wolf form and communicates with me telepathically. *How are you doing, Bray?*

I don't have the strength to respond. My head is

filled with thoughts of pain and anger. Does that tell him how I'm feeling? How much more explicit can I be?

It feels like an eternity passes between the time the moon wanes and the sun grows high in the sky. I want to sleep, but sometimes the process of my body healing is too much for me to sleep through. Healing at an accelerated pace, my ass. It feels like I'm stuck in a hospital bed getting drip-fed poison. My whole body feels like it's on fire.

Fausto returns with bandages. This time he stays in his human form while he tinkers with my legs. I expect pain to explode inside of me like a fireworks show, but these rockets are a bust—and I'm *thankful*. Instead of being enveloped in throbbing, stabbing, shooting sensations, I am treated to a dull roar.

"Your wounds are looking better today," Fausto announces as he wraps my legs again. "Another day and you'll probably be good as new."

Good as new? Who does he think I am? I'm not the type of person to rise from this bed and appreciate that I've been given another day to live. The second I'm able to get up, I'm storming the Cersei district. I'm killing everyone that I come across. Then when I find the fucking wolf that did this to me, I'm tearing him apart slowly limb from limb until he's a head on a spike watching his body burn to ash.

Revenge keeps me afloat. I drift from cloud to

cloud, imagining the blood I'll spill in retaliation. They won't see me coming. They won't expect a rabid, feral wolf to risk everything just for a little retribution.

Arcturus eventually comes to see me. He has a crutch stuck under his armpit and his face has faded bruises. He walks with a limp and I can't tell if it's because of his wounds or the crutch, maybe it's both. "I wanted to see how you're doing. Fausto says you won't talk to him."

It has nothing to do with Fausto and everything to do with making it through this hellish ordeal with my wits intact. If I succumb to the pain, I will lose my nerve. I will fear the suffering the mainlanders might inflict. I have to be hard if I'm going to heal properly. I can't risk a conversation with Fausto if he means to talk me down or ask me to wait.

"They got me pretty bad," Arcturus adds after a bit. He stalks around the room on his crutch until the sound is unbearable to my ears. Every stamp of his crutch on the stone floor drives me crazy. "I need to spend a few more hours in form if I want to get rid of this thing." He gestures toward the crutch before stopping at one of the windows and looking out onto the grounds below. "We're going to heal, you and me. Then we're going to get our revenge."

For the first time since I shifted and was brought to bed by Fausto, I raise my head from the mattress. I can't speak with Arcturus, my words are a whimper released from my muzzle, but he understands their meaning.

"We're going to bring Elspeth's father back here to watch us marry his daughter. I want him to watch his baby girl become ours." Arcturus' knuckles turn white as he grips the crutch harder. "If it wouldn't fuck her up beyond repair, I'd let him watch us deflower her." That would be one hell of a sight. I can only imagine the pain on Cason's face as we enter her one after the other.

Arcturus continues. "Instead, he can wait in a cell and watch as her belly gets bigger. He can waste away in her old cell. I want him to know what we've done to her. I want him to suffer as we've suffered. He'll never get to be a grandfather, not to our children."

I'm proud of him. These are thoughts that I've had in the long, aching moments of reality while waiting for my body to recover. I thought that this man was gone, that the Arcturus I'd known growing up had weakened under the strain of leadership. But he's proving me wrong.

Many years ago, Arcturus and I met on the playground. He and Fausto were already fast friends, a pair of wolf pups racing around playing tag. Each catch was succeeded by a nip and the two of them never got mad at one another. I wanted that and somehow Arcturus sensed it. He invited me into the fold and made sure that I didn't feel left out. He treated me like a younger brother; he treated me like *we* were brothers.

The years have made our bond stronger, but Arcturus, Fausto, and I are far from the kids we once were playing silly little games on the schoolyard. We have ambitions now; we have dreams. We have drifted from the things that brought us together all those years ago, but we still have a few things in common.

We will do anything to protect one another.

We will help each other no matter the cost.

And if a bully comes to our playground and wants to fight, we'll band together to make him regret standing up to us.

The landscape has changed but the rules are the same: if you fuck around, you're going to find out.

ELSPETH

I spend three days being treated by Levar before I'm released back to my cell. This time I'm given an oversized shirt to wear over my bandages. My stomach hurts with every step I take to the dungeon and my shoulder throbs, but the new prison guard is gentle with me.

He keeps an arm wrapped firmly around my waist and holds my hand as I take painful step after painful step. I almost expect him to tell me I'm doing a great job, but he isn't a fatherly figure. He may be nicer than the old guard, but he's a man of few words.

Rigo takes a peek in our direction when he hears us walking up. He takes in the sight of the guard's arm wrapped around me and the way he helps me gingerly sit down on my cot. This is enough to convince him to roll over onto his stomach and keep watching.

Bilia lies with her torso and head on the bed and her legs perpendicular on the wall. She offers a little show of interest but ultimately returns to staring at the ceiling; we do not entertain her.

When the guard is sure that I'm not going to fall off the bed and reopen a wound, he shuts the door behind me and locks it with the keys jingling around his waistband before walking back to his post.

"Who's the new guy?" I ask when I'm certain he's out of earshot.

Bilia kicks one ankle over the other to cross them against the wall. "I don't know. He didn't introduce himself. Maybe I'll ask at the next prison-guard mixer." She must be in good spirits if she has enough energy to muster up some sarcasm.

"What the hell happened?" Rigo wears a glare and curiosity at the same time. "One minute you'd gone upstairs and the next it sounded like a battle was waging in the castle. The guard locked the dungeon against intruders, but most of us have ears. The prisoners went nuts. I heard some guy at the other end of the dungeon slammed his head into the wall over and over again until he passed out and bled to death."

I want to say that at least he was responsible for his own death, but that's not true. Being held captive in this dungeon and being tortured on a regular basis probably drove the prisoner insane. He might have been the one to ultimately inflict his final blow, but he wasn't in his right mind. "Just another reason to hate the Kings," I mumble under my breath.

Rigo is unimpressed. "Do you think this is a joke?" He gets up from his favorite spot in the cell and walks toward the bars. "What happened up there? Why have you been gone for so long?"

I wish I was gone longer, frankly. Levar might have only fed me soup and rice, but it was better than the swill I was dining on down here. I had endless access to all the water my stomach could hold and I used a toilet that didn't threaten to back up and overflow if I jiggled the handle incorrectly.

"Hello?" He raises his voice. "Answer me!"

"I don't know what happened," I snap. "I was screaming bloody murder while those animals carved their initials into my chest when the door busted open and a pack of wolves showed up. I'm *told* that my home district launched a counterattack to get me back, but I'm also told that if retrieval was unsuccessful, they were ordered to kill me instead. I don't know what happened because I passed out from blood loss when someone sunk their teeth into my kidney."

I can't explain how angry I am about this whole situation. I don't know what's true and what's a lie that was fed to me by the Kings to make me come around to their way of thinking. I thought at first there wasn't even an attack, but Levar assured me that he was taking care of a dozen people throughout the castle who'd gotten in the intruders' way.

"They can't have you back," Rigo argues with a frown. "You don't belong to them. They shouldn't have done that."

I look up from the floor and make eye contact with him. "What?" I reply sharply.

He is patient when he explains to me that I'm Alize Nikae's granddaughter. "You belong in the Forbidden Lands. Maybe you are not the shifter that she was," Rigo allows, "but this is your home. This is where you should have been born."

Now I wish I could bang my head into the wall until I pass out and bleed to death. "It was a mistake telling you why I'm here," I grumble to myself, feeling frustrated by all men in my life. The Mad Kings for kidnapping me. My father for not warning me what might happen. My cellmate for trying to gaslight me into believing that this is my true home.

Bilia, who wasn't awake when I told Rigo who I was before, turns her head sideways to look at me. "You're a Nikae?" She wrinkles her nose in disgust as she stares. "You're kind of scrawny to be a wolf shifter."

I grit my teeth and talk myself out of screaming at her. *Be calm. Keep it together.* "I'm not a shifter. I'm a witch."

She snorts at me and then goes back to staring at

the ceiling. "Yeah, right," Bilia responds in derision. "*I'm* a witch. A damn good one at that and it's why they've got this fucking dog collar on me." She screams the dog collar part and a few people from down the hall start piping up in response. "You're not a witch, honey, or else you'd be wearing an accessory, too."

Now that I think about it, I would have preferred to die in the counterattack. If my burst kidney had done its job, maybe I wouldn't be sitting in this dingy dungeon trying to defend myself against crazy people. People who performed criminal actions, nonetheless. Despite their current circumstances, they tried to overthrow and murder a King. I'm above these people. I'm better than them because I'm innocent. I shouldn't have to answer to them.

"You just wait," Rigo promises, "you're going to come to terms with who you are eventually. Then it'll seem crazy that you ever wanted to leave."

Maybe if I get a lobotomy in the near future. Though considering the men holding me captive, I wouldn't be surprised if they attempted one.

I grab a blanket that's been doubling as a pillow and drape it over the lower half of my body. It isn't much, but it keeps my bare legs warm while I ignore Rigo and contemplate if I'll ever get out of here alive.

Bilia starts singing a song that I've never heard before. Her voice echoes through the dungeon, twisting and turning down all the hallways until all anyone can hear are the words of her song. It stirs anger in the other prisoners, but it lulls me to sleep.

Darkness, darkness, disappear
My heart can't handle when you're near
Slowly, slowly, drift away
And bring about a better day

I fall into a dreamless sleep and when I'm awoken several hours later, it's because the Mad Kings are in my cell. Darkness did not go away; it only brought more darkness.

ELSPETH

"It's been years since I've been down here," Arcturus announces with a sneer. "It's much dingier than I anticipated."

The sound of his voice mixed with the metal door scraping along the floor jolts me from my slumber. The three Kings walk into my cell making the already small space feel even smaller. Arcturus is so tall that his head almost brushes the seven-foot ceilings.

Fausto looks at my toilet as if it's a suspect in a crime. "The doesn't look sanitary," he mumbles to himself.

Much like when Bray came to visit me, I reckon this is the first time either of the other two has been to the dungeons. They might house their prisoners down here, but they don't visit for giggles.

"Welcome to my humble abode," I yawn midway

through the sentence. I think my body hurts more now than when I came downstairs a few hours ago. "Please, take a seat anywhere."

Out of the corner of my eye, I catch Rigo watching us. He doesn't hide behind the pretense of reading his book; he might miss some of the action if he's holding a paperback in front of his face.

"I think I'll stand, but thanks for your *hospitality*." Arcturus looks disgusted to be here. Wait until he finds out about the food, the overflowing toilets, and the lack of showers. It'll be a real turn-on when he touches me next and gets a whiff of what he's been subjecting me to.

"We came for a couple of reasons. One was to check on you." Bray is carefully restraining his anger, but it's visible from the clenched fists and the knot his jaw where he's grinding his teeth together.

I look down at my body and then back up at the Mad Kings. If someone didn't know any better, they'd think that I looked relatively fine. The shirt that Levar gave me covers all my bandages, but not all the scrapes and bruises. My arms are littered with varying shades of blue and purple. A patch of skin on my thigh looks like road rash from being drug across the ground. I have two broken toes, both of which have turned a nasty shade, but otherwise, I don't look half bad.

"The other is to allow you to speak to the prisoner," Arcturus adds.

Confusion swallows me whole as a frown forms on my face. "What prisoner?" I thought *I* was the prisoner. I guess there are others around me, but besides Rigo and Bilia, I don't know what they're here for.

Fausto bends down to remove the blanket from my lap and offers me both his hands. "I'll help you up," he insists quietly. I reluctantly place my hands in his and hiss through the pain as I get to my feet.

"While none of our men were killed during the raid, four of your father's were. One was left for dead, but he pulled through and we've been keeping him locked in the room at the top of the stairs. Now that you're well enough," Arcturus emphasizes well *enough*, "we want you to talk to him."

I'm almost excited. This is someone from my home district, someone who came here to save me. I can ask him point blank if the Kings are lying about my father wanting me dead. He'll show them, he'll show everyone. My father would never want me to die. "Sure. Take me to him." I try to hide my excitement but I don't think I do the best job of it. I'm nearly bounding out of the cell with Fausto's help.

The door is left open behind us as they lead me forward. Arcturus is in front, forcing himself to take smaller steps so he doesn't disappear from our sight.

He casts an occasional glance behind him to make sure that we're still coming.

Fausto and Bray share the space on my back, each wrapping an arm around me to hold me aloft. I think if I stopped walking, they would happily carry me up the stairs to the room at the top.

"There we go," Fausto mumbles as I make it to the final step. "While we're here, we might get Levar to check those bandages."

It's only been a few hours since I last saw the doctor, but the strain of walking up and down the stairs has caused the wound to reopen. Fausto peers under my shirt to examine the pristine white bandages that are slowly turning pink. I want to slap his hands away and tell him to leave me alone, but I suck it up and let him do his inspection.

"This one looks like it's healing well," he says as he eyes the smaller dressing above my heart.

I'm scared to have that one removed. For the rest of my life, I'll have their initials carved into my flesh. It's an embarrassment.

Arcturus calls the guard to unlock the door. "Don't try anything," he warns as we wait. "This man will not be able to help you. If he tries, he'll die and you'll be punished."

What more can they do to me? They've dislocated my shoulder and put their mark on my body. What comes next? Taking an arm? Removing a leg?

Regardless, I nod my head in agreement. I'll say whatever they want to hear if it means speaking to a soldier of my father's. It'll be like a little taste of home.

Except the room where he's being kept is even worse than my prison cell. There are no windows and the lights are shut off when we enter. The guard flips a switch and the man chained to the wall hisses in response. I hear his shackles clang against the stone as he tries to protect his eyes from the light.

"Garth," I breathe, recognizing the head of my father's security team. He's the last person I would have expected to be caught.

"Careful," Arcturus warns as I start to get closer, "he's dangerous."

I'd call Garth Hessket a lot of things, but not dangerous, not to me. He's been like an uncle to me for as long as I can remember. He taught me self-defense when I was young and showed me how to shoot a gun, use a bow and arrow, and how to hunt for my own food. I don't remember half of the skills he taught me, but I think if I had to survive off the land, I might be able to hobble my way along with what I can recall.

Garth looks exhausted. He hangs from his wrists on the wall, his face bloody and bruised from the fight a few days before. He doesn't have any visible wounds or marks, at least not any that seem life-threatening. When he catches sight of me, Garth narrows his eyes.

"You're supposed to be dead," he whispers, the echo of his words bouncing off the walls.

My jaw drops. Could everything Fausto told me be true? Did my father really send his men to the Forbidden Lands to kill his daughter?

FAUSTO

W e've already spoken to Garth, a handful
of times, actually. He spit on us, swore at
us, and refused to tell us what he knows. It
was Bray's idea to get Elspeth.

"She probably knows the guy, or at least knows *of*
him," Bray explained. "Maybe she can crack him."

I didn't have any high hopes that she'd be the key
to unlocking the vault of Garth Hessket, but she seems
to be proving me wrong. Of course, she falls apart
when he starts telling her the truth.

"You're his pride and joy, you know," Garth tells
her. He looks angry to see her knowing that he failed
his job. "Your father knew they'd come for you one
day. He just didn't expect them to succeed." He looks
to Arcturus when he says that last part and venom
seeps into his tone and gaze.

Arcturus snorts in derision as he walks over to the table and chairs in the corner of the room. He takes a seat and kicks his feet up. "That's why she's ours now. I'd have you relay that to your master, but I don't think you're going to make it home."

Garth fights against the chains holding him to the wall. He might bare his teeth, but he can't shift with the magic-absorbing collar around his neck. He acts like the animal he is when he's a wolf, but he looks pathetic instead of threatening. "You sick banished fucks," he swears again. "You will rue the day that you stole from the Avermos. Cason will make you regret taking his daughter."

Bray gets in Garth's face. He hovers over him by several inches and he isn't afraid to spit back at the man. "He'll regret bringing you here when we send your body back to him one piece at a fucking time. We'll start with your fingers and toes. A few small gifts to warm him up to what's coming." Bray grabs Garth's chin and digs his fingers into the bone. "Then we'll send him bigger pieces, like your fucking leg and that inchworm you call a cock."

This is the first time I've seen Garth cower in fear. Even though I've visited him multiple times per day and Arcturus and Bray have been by a few times since rising from their deathbeds, he's been as hard as steel. But with a credible threat on the table, he looks like he's been thrown off his game.

"Bray, please," Elspeth begs in the silence. "I need to ask him something."

The desperation in her tone tugs at the strings of my heart. If it was up to me, I'd step back and let her have her way. But Bray stands there for a few more moments clenching and unclenching his fists as he tries to decide if he's going to slam his knuckles into Garth's face. He's done it already, hence the blood practically coating the man's mouth. But he lets his anger subside long enough to pivot to the side and give Elspeth access to him. "Make it fast," he growls as he crosses his arms over his chest.

I follow Elspeth from behind as she steps closer to the chained man. Her breaths are shallow courtesy of the pain that she's in. If she could shift, she could heal herself, but we never got around to a second lesson. "You said I should be dead." There is apprehension in her tone; she's unsure of herself. "What did you mean?" Or perhaps she's unsure that she wants to hear the answer.

Garth avoids meeting Elspeth's eyes. He looks at the hem of her shirt, grazing her bare thighs with his gaze as she stands before him. "It wasn't my idea," he mutters.

"What idea?" She takes a step closer. At this range, he could kick her if he wanted to. His feet aren't tied up. "Garth, please. You've been like family to me."

"I *am* family to you," he swears. "Your father is my

pack leader. I protect what is his and he protects me. We are bonded in a way that you will never understand." Garth hardens himself against the task coming next. When he looks up to meet Elspeth's eyes, he's practically ice. "Your father loves you, Elspeth, and he'd do anything to keep you safe. Even," he trails off. No matter how hard he makes himself, he can't bring himself to say what we all know to be true.

Elspeth must realize that. I watch from behind as her body language changes. Despite the loss of a kidney and several other minor injuries, she straightens her spine until she seems like she's a foot taller. Elspeth squares her shoulders and pulls them back to puff out of her chest. "Even kill his own daughter," she finishes for him.

Garth looks miserable, but he nods his head in solemn agreement. "He didn't want you kidnapped, raped, and forced to become their prisoner. He didn't want you to be like this." All he has is his chin to gesture with, but he points it at Elspeth anyway. "He wanted you to be free whether it was back home with your family or somewhere in the great beyond."

The shallow breaths become deeper. Elspeth takes another step forward and out of reflex, I take a step toward her. If Garth tries anything, I want to be close enough to jump into action. But it's Elspeth that brings up her hand and slaps Garth across the face before I realize what's happening.

"I trusted you." Her voice is small like a child's. "I believed that you would protect me all of my life."

"It's not that simple," Garth protests. "I was just following orders."

Elspeth hits him again, this time with her other hand. She winces in pain but that doesn't stop her. "Orders to kill me."

He takes her abuse more quietly than he took ours. When Bray struck him in the face, he became a spitting, angry beast. I suspect he feels genuinely bad about what he's done to Elspeth. "I asked to be the one to do it." His words come out barely above a whisper. "I knew that if I could get to you, I could do it without hurting you."

"It was you," Elspeth realizes. "You were the one latched onto me."

Garth looks at Bray. "I was going to do it humanely, make sure that you didn't die in pain. But then *he* got in the way."

Bray reaches forward and grabs Garth around the throat. He presses his fingertips into the skin as the prisoner gasps for air. "You were foolish to think that you'd take her from me. All you did was injure her."

Shockingly, Elspeth reaches up to place her hand on Bray's arm. Her fingers look tiny wrapped around his wrist. "Don't. I have to say something."

Once more she transforms. The way she pulls herself together when she expects a fight is riveting to see. Bray withdraws his arm but he looks unhappy about it.

"In the couple of weeks that I've been here, I've fought the Mad Kings at every turn. Every time they told me who I was, I got angry. Every time they tried to convince me I had magic, it upset me. They kept saying I was a Queen, a woman born to a bloodline more powerful than I could ever imagine." Elspeth starts stepping away from Garth. There is no anger in her voice, no malice toward the man before her, just recognition. "It took me a while to realize that while they built me up, my father tore me down. I don't even think I realized it until just now. My family has been telling me for years that I don't have any power, that I am weak, that I don't even have what it takes to go to a proper academy."

Our time has come. Finally. I don't even care that she called us by that sick moniker we've been given by the mainlanders.

"I believed that I was worthless, just like they said I was. But that must not be the truth if my father was willing to risk his men and my life in order to keep the Kings from having control of me." She keeps backing up until she runs into me. Elspeth jumps a little from the unexpected touch but keeps her eyes on Garth. "Which begs the question, why would my family make me feel powerless and useless if I wasn't? Who does that to their own flesh and blood?"

When Elspeth's voice breaks, I place a supportive hand on her hip. I want to tell her to keep going, to say how she really feels, but I'm afraid if I intervene, she'll lose steam.

Garth opens his mouth to respond and Elspeth cuts him off. "When it came to choosing between watching me die and risking their lives to keep me alive, the Mad Kings did what you couldn't. They protected me and kept me safe. They chose me."

Arcturus proudly stands at attention. He wears a cat ate the canary grin as he looks at the detained prisoner.

"It's a good thing you didn't save me, Garth, because I didn't need saving. I think I'm exactly where I'm supposed to be."

A choir of angels could descend from the heavens and start singing a hallelujah chorus and it wouldn't be half as spectacular hearing those words from come Elspeth's lips.

ELSPETH

They don't take me back to my prison cell.
Instead, I am transported to the third floor.
Arcturus carries me up the additional two
flights of stairs while sending Fausto to fetch the
doctor. Bray clears the way and opens a door when we
reach the end of a hallway. They could drop me off
here and let the labyrinth of corridors and entrances
imprison me in the castle. I lost track of how I'd gotten
here five turns ago.

The room we enter is large and covered in
windows. The natural light beaming in through the
panes of glass makes my heart feel light. I try to look at
everything all at once, craning my neck one way and
then the other. I catch a glimpse of two doors leading
away from the main room, a large wardrobe pressed
up against the wall, a sitting area right in front of a

fire, and more. It is a grand room, a room fit for a Queen if I had to guess.

Arcturus is gentle as he places me on the large bed. The silky soft comforter feels like heaven on my skin. Having an actual mattress beneath me is almost enough to lull me to sleep. but the voices of the men that brought me here keep me awake.

"We can trust you, right?" Arcturus asks as he backs away a few feet. For the first time since I met him, he looks apprehensive. "You won't run?"

I couldn't run even if I wanted to. I could barely hobble up and down the stairs without feeling like someone was repeatedly jamming a fork into my side. But I know what he's asking. It isn't about whether I can actually run, it's about if I want to. "I won't lie, it crossed my mind to remember the exact steps of how you brought me here so that I could retrace them if I wanted to leave. But even if I hadn't gotten lost a few minutes ago, I don't know if I *would* have left."

Bray breathes a sigh of relief before perching himself at the foot of the bed. He leans up against a column on the four-poster bed frame and kicks his feet up parallel to me. "I was hoping you might say that. I'd hate to have to chase you down if you run. You don't want to find out what would happen to you if I caught you trying to escape."

The truth is that seeing Garth was what should have happened from the beginning. Imprisoning me in a dark, dirty dungeon and inflicting cruel punishment on me would have worked eventually, but it was much quicker to bring in someone I knew that could tell me the truth. Or at least bits and pieces of it. There is a chance that I might never know the whole story from my parents' point of view. I just have the Mad Kings' version to go off of.

"Through there," Arcturus points to an oversized door in the corner of the room, "is your on-suite. We will need to get you some new clothes, feminine amenities, shoes, whatever you'd like, but we can take that one step at a time." He turns his body in the other direction and points toward the other door in the room. "That leads to my room. As the Queen, you are accessible to the first point of the crown at all times. Bray's room is across the hall and Fausto's room was the first we passed in this wing. This wing is where the royals live."

Is it wrong that I'm excited to be here? I haven't moved an inch since Arcturus set me down on the bed. There are half a dozen pillows neatly stacked that I lean up against. Everything smells fresh and clean. The fear that these men will break my arm or force me to do something against my will seems to be receding with every kind word that they say. In short, this place is paradise considering where I just came from.

A knock at the half-open door draws our attention; Fausto stands there with Levar in tow. The doctor carries a black medical bag and is quick to make his way over to me. "I thought I warned them not to have you moving around too much," he mumbles as he lifts my shirt and starts working on the pink bandage. While he carefully removes the soiled dressings, he shakes his head in disgust. "We could use one of the healers. Preferably a witch."

"Aren't *you* a witch?" Bray asks with a sneer.

Levar looks up from the gaping wound on the right side of my stomach to make eye contact with Bray. Very matter-of-factly, he says, "This girl seems to have made the three of you more sensitive, but she hasn't knocked the asshole out of you yet." I'm stunned that he has the audacity to speak to the Mad Kings like this. "I am a *wizard*, yes. I stopped her internal bleeding and cured the infection from the bite. But the wound needs to be manually stitched together or someone with a deeper understanding of shifter skin needs to be brought in to close the wound. Since old age brings frailty—something I expect the three of you will never understand given your penchant for bringing trouble to the castle—my hands are not what they used to be. I cannot stitch or close these bites."

"I could do it," I offer. "I've stitched up a lot of people back home." There isn't enough time for the tension in the room to build over Levar's disrespectful assessments. Everyone turns to look at me in surprise. "I'll just need some local anesthesia, probably." I look down at the two gaping bite marks left by Garth's canines. While a handful of tiny marks dot my stomach from his teeth, it's the canines that have left the biggest wounds. "They'll probably need less than a dozen stitches each. It won't take long." Silence follows my offer.

My parents might not have encouraged me to become a shifter like them, but they were happy to have me learn how to heal others without magic. It's a skill often left to humans, I've heard. They put people in machines to find out what's wrong with them and use medical equipment to treat certain conditions. Doctors in the human world heal with medicine and manual practices, whereas witches and wizards in Meira'mor use their hands and the magic they were born with to piece people back together.

"Is that a good idea, doc?" Arcturus asks Levar after a few moments. "Should she be stitching herself up?" He inquires as if I'm not here listening to them.

"I've done it before," I butt it with a glare. "I busted my knee open when I was twelve and I stitched it back together without my parents ever noticing." I point at a silvery-white scar on my knee that travels diagonally across the cap. "And I didn't even have local anesthesia. I just bit down on a stick and did it."

Bray raises an eyebrow and looks at Fausto and Arcturus. "Damn. She's tough."

I don't know if tough is the word I'd use; I was

mainly trying not to get in trouble with my parents. That was just a couple of years before they gave up on me becoming a wolf shifter like them and everything I did seemed to set them off. I didn't want to walk home with a bloody, busted knee and have to listen to them lecture me about safety when I could just take care of it myself.

"Levar, you got local anesthesia?" Fausto walks over to take a closer look at the bite marks on my stomach. They are pretty gnarly and a shiver of disgust races down his spine.

Bray snorts while calling him a pussy. "You've done worse to others," he adds with a shake of his head.

Fausto glares at his friend and explains that it's different. "I try not to inflict those kinds of wounds on people that I care about."

I didn't realize that they cared about me. Not in that fashion, anyway. They said that they'd kidnapped me to make me their Queen and to steal back what was rightfully theirs. I was beginning to think of it as an arranged marriage to three men who've likely murdered more people than I've saved. We might one day come to a gracious understanding that we are equals, but I didn't expect them to truly *care*.

"I'll go get the supplies," Levar interrupts. "But if you start losing too much blood or you look like you might pass out, I'm going to stop you and these bozos will have to find a real healer."

I stifle a grin as the doctor momentarily leaves the room. "I'm surprised that you let him speak to you guys like that." If I'd have dared to say half the disrespectful things Levar did, I think I'd find myself back in my prison cell chatting the day away with Rigo and Bilia.

Arcturus looks at the door that Levar just left through. I can see on his face that he rejects half a dozen explanations before coming back with the one that makes the most sense. "We classify people into different boxes out here in the Forbidden Lands. There are people you *need* around you, there are people you *want* around you, and there are people that simply *exist* around you." When he drags his dark gaze back to me, it's with a shrug and purse of his lips. "Levar is all of those people at once. We need him because of his expertise and we want him around because he's seen things that we could only ever dream of. But at the same time, he's just *here* and we have to put up with it. We can't get rid of him and we can't risk his life because we need him. We also wouldn't want to because he's one of the best wizards there is out here. There are a few witches in other parts of the Forbidden Lands that can do what he does," Arcturus pauses, "but they generally require a substantial payment if asked to provide services."

I nod my head absentmindedly as he speaks. Levar sounds like a very important person and that's why he's allowed to get away with snarky little comments and disrespect. Which begs the question: if Levar is so important, what does that make me? And what can I get away with if I try hard enough?

ELSPETH

The difference between being housed on the castle's third floor versus the dungeon is like the difference between night and day. I can't even count the ways my life has improved since moving into the hall of royalty, as the Mad Kings call it.

The first thing I did was take an hour-long shower. Levar warned me against it saying that my bandages would have to be changed again. Despite stitching up the skin with less-than-perfect results, he had replaced the dressings with fresh ones. I immediately soiled those with soap and water.

"There have been a few queens since Alize was taken," Bray droned on while Arcturus and Fausto helped me to the bathroom and carefully undressed me. "This room is stocked with items from the last

Queen. You are free to use whatever you'd like. The Master of the house will be by at some point in the next week to take inventory of your preferences in dining and personal items, among other things."

Arcturus pulled my shirt off and I stood before the three of them wearing only pristine white swathes of gauze on my shoulder and across my stomach. A shiver raced down my spine and I turned my back to the three kings before I could crumble in vulnerability. "Do-do I get a little privacy?"

The three mumbled their ascent before departing. I was left alone with the shower, a rack full of body soaps and scrubs, and five different kinds of hair products. It was one of the most relaxing showers of my life.

Watching the dirt spill from my body and wash down the drain felt like being reborn. I hadn't realized I was wearing a layer of grime until the soap washed it away. I found micro-abrasions on the bottom of my feet as suds filled the crevices they created and left me wincing in pain. But after a few minutes, the sharpness of the now-cleaned cuts receded and I was able to relax beneath the jets of water.

When I had gained a little more strength back, I pulled the bandage off my shoulder to reveal the initials carved into my skin. AFB. The flesh would heal in time, but the scars would be left on my body forever.

It occurred to me half a dozen times over the following week to ask what happened to the Kings and Queen before us. Why would someone leave behind all their products? Why are the Kings so young? If the previous rulers were decided on based on the Queen's oldest daughter taking a pack, then what happened after Alize Nikae was kidnapped? Arcturus, Bray, and Fausto took the throne without a wife by their side. How did it happen?

I had a lot of questions, but I didn't have the courage to ask them. I let the Kings show and tell me what they wanted me to know. I'd narrowly escaped spending the rest of my life living in a dungeon getting regularly tortured. I could be grateful for the soft bed I now slept on and the delicious food available to me at all hours of the day.

In their quest to teach me what it meant to be a Queen of the Forbidden Lands, I spent night and day learning from the Kings.

Arcturus was determined to bring out the wolf inside of me. He swore that he would strip away a decade of verbal abuse and teach me how to shift no matter what it took. Sometimes I felt nothing but frustration, but some days I felt a tingling in my extremities that gave me hope.

Fausto educated me on the history of the Forbidden Lands, from when they came into existence until the day they'd met me. I had spent my life taking a backseat to the men in the Cersei district, but Fausto swore that wouldn't be the same here. He said that I would be immortalized in the history books and my story would inspire little girls everywhere. I learned more from him than I remembered learning back home.

Bray was gone during the days, but when he returned at dinner time, he spent hours afterward showing me around the castle and community. I learned the names of the men and women that sat on the Kings' council. I was starting to find my way from my room to the kitchen without having to ask for help. I was even allowed to leave the castle. With a guard by my side, of course.

The Forbidden Lands were different than I expected them to be. With darkness acting as a curtain on the plains as I was brought here, I didn't see much of the place that I now called home. In the daylight, it looked less like the war zone I expected in my mind and more like the Cersei district.

People lived in nice homes, but Bray told me that they worked hard to build them from the ground up. "When someone is ready to leave home, it's a family tradition to gather materials and build their home in the weeks leading up to their departure. Land is traded and materials are bartered for. When someone dies, their home is passed onto a relative or friend. There is no buying and selling in the Forbidden Lands, not in the traditional sense. Our existence doesn't depend on how many gold coins someone has in their pocket."

Life seemed simpler out here. Everyone went to the same school and was taught the same basic principles of history, magic, and community. While a majority of the residents of the Forbidden Lands were wolf shifters, Bray informed me that there were clusters of other beings in the surrounding areas. The furthest from the Meira'mor that I knew were witches and wizards. Far to the east were the dragon and bear shifters that carved out their existence in a way that didn't offend. Demons scoured the lands with their succubus lovers and mated like rabbits. The rules of the mainland did not govern these people.

O n an idle afternoon when the Mad Kings are gone on a mission, Roth walks with me through the streets. He does his best to fill Bray's shoes by showing me where different packs live and how they support the Forbidden Lands. It is only after a long silence that he breaks from tradition.

"You may miss your family back home. You may miss the life you once led. But I promise you, you will come to love the Forbidden Lands. You will find that it is truly where you belong." He has remained impartial and informative during our other expeditions, but I appreciate his plain speaking.

The truth is that I don't miss my family or my life before. If I'm being honest with myself, I'm unsure of what to think about it. The woman I used to be didn't actually exist; she was a lie told to me by the people I loved and trusted most.

The Mad Kings might have brought me here against my will, but they did it for my benefit. They did it to make me the woman I was born to be.

BRAY

I said that I'd get my revenge and I will. But Arcturus doesn't want me to stalk through the Cersei district killing everyone that crosses my path. "Have a little more discretion," were the words he used, if I remember correctly. I wonder how discreet it will seem when I return to the castle with Cason fucking Avermo bleeding out of every hole I can put in his body.

Breathe, I tell myself. I will be able to inflict the most damage if I take my time, gauge the danger, and attack at the right moment. *Don't get careless.*

I lie in wait for a few minutes longer. People of all ages and races pass by me. With the sun high in the sky, I'm risking my life doing this in broad daylight. But Cason must pay for the sins of his soldiers. I may never find the guard that tried to maim me, but I'll take it out on Elspeth's father.

I've been watching him for a few days now. Cason has a pattern of behavior that's as easy to predict as the rise and fall of the moon. He gets up at the same time every morning and is home for approximately an hour getting dressed, making breakfast, and gathering his things for the day. After that, he drives downtown to his office. Somehow he owns the largest building in the Cersei district. Nobody owns buildings that large without doing something nefarious to get them. Call it cynicism or call it truth; this man has broken a few rules to be in power, I just know it.

Cason usually spends a few hours in the morning meeting with people. He takes his lunch at the same time and same place every day. Sometimes his wife joins him, other times he's alone. People walk by his table and ask him how work is going or how the family is, but no one ever asks about Elspeth. It makes me wonder what part she played in his world.

The rest of Cason's day is spent in his office. He bounces between paperwork and more meetings. Since I can't listen in, I don't know what these meetings consist of. I try to pry that information out of Elspeth gently, but she only shrugs and tells me that he works in finance.

Finance positions don't exist in the Forbidden Lands. They could if we cared more about currency, but we only use gold coins and a few paper bills when we're purchasing from a bar or restaurant. The owners tend to need the money to buy wares from the surrounding districts. They assimilate well into Meira'mor's mainland, but only long enough to make purchases and get what they need before getting out.

At 4:30 pm sharp every day, Cason packs up his things and leaves for home. I don't follow him there because that's not where I'm going to corner him. He has guards at his home. It was difficult enough getting Elspeth out; I'm not even going to attempt to kidnap Cason from there.

Over a week has passed since I started watching Cason's every move. It doesn't seem like enough time to know this man's schedule in and out, but he's so damn boring that I can't wait any longer. It has to be today. Or tomorrow. Or the day after that. If I don't capture him soon, I'm going to blow my brains out while wasting away in routine.

I wait until lunchtime before I make my move. Cason leaves his office at precisely 12:30 and walks half a block to a deli where he orders half a sandwich, a cup of soup, and a small bowl of fruit. Sometimes he switches out the fruit for chips, but for the most part, he's a relatively healthy guy.

I wait to see if anyone is going to join him, but the booth stays empty after ten minutes. Cason enjoys his lunch with the newspaper beside him. His eyes scan the tiny print as his fingers idly play with the spoon sticking out of his soup cup.

When I'm certain that no one is going to interrupt our lunch, I leave my table by the door and join Cason in the booth. He is surprised when he looks up to see me sitting in front of him. "Hello?" He greets with a tilt of his head in confusion. "Can I help you with something?"

He can help me with a lot of things if I'm being honest. He can help me by pointing me in the direction of the shifter that tried to kill me. He can help me by calling his goons off trying to steal Elspeth back. He can help me by getting into the van I have parked at the edge of town and quietly coming back to the castle with me. But I start off with the simplest thing he can do to help me. "Are you Cason Avermo?" Which is to answer my questions.

Cason grabs the napkin in his lap and brings it to his lips, daintily dabbing away invisible mustard. "I am. Is there something I can do for you?" He asks again.

I lean back in the seat with a cat-ate-the-canary grin and cross my arms over my chest. "You can do a lot for me, Cason. You can finish your lunch and then follow me back to my car, for starters."

A humorous expression appears on his face. "Oh, really?" He's unable to keep the amusement out of his tone. "And why would I do that?"

I want to grab him by that high-necked, stupid shirt of his and pull him toward me. I want to see the look in his eyes turn to fear when I bare my teeth and tell him that if he doesn't do as I say, I'll kill him right here, right now.

I have to settle for returning his tone with a chuckle of my own. "Because I'm going to take you to your daughter. And if you're nice enough about it, I won't bring you to her bloody and beaten to a pulp."

The smile on Cason's face disappears, replaced with a hard, stony look. "You're from *there*, aren't you?" He asks in a low voice.

"There?" I repeat back to him with a sneer. "You mean the Forbidden Lands? The place the outcasts live? The one you recently raided in an attempt to kill the Kings and your daughter?"

Cason slams the napkin down on the table bringing half a dozen eyes sprawling in our direction. "I didn't try to kill my daughter," he growls between gritted teeth. "I was trying to save her."

I sigh in annoyance and shake my head. Cason is such a well-put-together man. He comes to work every day in nice black slacks and a white button-up shirt. The shine on his shoes is bright enough to blind someone. It's funny to watch a man like that lose his temper. "Interesting, because I tried to save Elspeth, too. The only difference between your version of *saving her* and mine is that *I'm* not the one who punctured her kidney and put her in the hospital for three days."

His face is devoid of color. Cason's jaw drops and he sits across from me speechless.

"Are you surprised that she got hurt or surprised that she's still alive?" All traces of humor are gone from my tone as I cross-examine him. "We know what your plan was, Cason. We've got one of your men locked up in the dungeon back home. He sang like a fucking canary. But hey, when you peel off a man's finger and toenails one by one before sprinkling salt on the open wounds, it's hard not to tell your torturers all your secrets."

Cason is a sickly pale color and I almost feel bad for him. He's probably imagining all the terrible things I've done to his soldier and his daughter. "Does Elspeth know?" He asks quietly after a minute.

"Know what?"

He takes a deep breath and leans closer to me until the table is pressing into his stomach. "Does Elspeth know that Garth Hessket is imprisoned?"

I can't help but laugh. The eyes that were watching us before surreptitiously return as the chortle garners their attention once more. "Elspeth's talked to your guy. She knows about the whole *'if you can't take her alive, leave her dead'* thing. How'd you know it was him, by the way?"

Cason narrows his eyes at me before leaning back

in his seat. "He's part of my pack. I could feel his presence even as I left the castle. It took hours before the connection was lost and it wasn't because he died. We lost a few good men that day, but Garth was the best of them."

Could have fooled me. Garth was sent on a suicidal mission to kill the Queen of the Forbidden Lands. She might not be crowned yet and no one else may know who she is, but killing her would have resulted in a war. "If it makes you feel any better, Elspeth knows everything. In fact, finding out that you sent your best hitman to kill her did what the Kings and I couldn't: it convinced her to trust that we had her best interests at heart."

The man sitting across from me looks murderous. "I swear to God if you laid a finger on her," he threatens.

"You'll what?" I growl. "I'll fucking end you, Cason. I'll do it right here in front of all your little friends and acquaintances. Just try me."

Cason's jaw tightens. Silence reigns across the table. Tension rises like a tidal wave. "Fine. Let's go to your car."

A smile replaces the scowl on my face. "Fantastic," I announce with delight. "You're more amenable than I expected you to be! I thought I'd have to break a few bones. Which, now that I think about it," I frown, "it's a disappointment that I didn't get to. But no matter." I look at his half-eaten lunch and gesture my hand at the plate. "Would you like to finish?"

He pushes the food away from him with a disgusted look on his face. "I've lost my appetite."

Pity. That's probably the last good meal he'll ever have.

ELSPETH

"This is stupid." I open my eyes and I'm immediately met with Arcturus and Fausto's glares. "What?" I return their looks. "I feel stupid."

Arcturus paces around the room with his hands pulled behind his back. "You're not taking this seriously, Elspeth," he chides.

I look around as if to ask him what the hell this all means if I'm not taking it seriously. I'm naked, in a bathtub, listening to soothing music, and trying to meditate myself into being a wolf shifter. What part of me isn't taking this seriously?

"Maybe you aren't relaxed enough. We should get some candles," Fausto says excitedly. "Do you want a warm beverage?"

Arcturus looks murderous. "I don't think burning some fucking sage is going to help, Fausto."

Fausto rolls his eyes when his friend's back is turned. "Whatever," he mumbles under his breath, flipping him the middle finger in the process.

I feel out of my depth and it isn't just because I'm naked in front of these men. There's a lot of pressure on me to become someone I gave up on long ago. I was born to be a wolf shifter like my parents and my parent's parents before them, but when you fail to achieve your birthright, it's emotionally damaging. Being asked to fail repeatedly in front of two more watchful, waiting wolves makes me even more anxious.

I sink further into the bath until the water is up to my chin. My hair is piled high on my head in a clip to avoid getting wet, but the strands that escape stick to my damp skin. "What if it never happens?" The vibrations from my voice cause tiny waves to ripple away from me.

Arcturus stops pacing. I see the concern written on his features as he asks himself this question over and over again. *What if she never awakens? What if she isn't the wolf shifter we thought she was? What if we stole her and put in all this work for nothing?* Whatever the answer to those questions, Arcturus shakes them off. "You are still the Queen, Elspeth. It doesn't matter if you can shift or not." There is no indecision or anger in his tone; he truly believes what he's saying.

But does he mean it? And if he does, will the rest of the packs and people that live in the Forbidden Lands accept me? I'd be the first Nikae in centuries to let down my ancestors by being devoid of magical ability. There would be no reason for the dwellers of this outcast district to follow me. There'd be no reason for Arcturus, Fausto, or Bray to mate with me when there's a high chance that my failed genetics could pass on to our children and they'd be magicless, too.

I've come a long way from my initial thinking that I might somehow climb the bars that enclose the castle and escape back to the Cersei district. Thinking about having the Mad Kings' children is a whole new realm for me. But all of this is.

I have the amenities of my home. I am more protected than I've ever been before. I am treated like royalty. But what if that all disappears if I can't be the woman they need me to be?

"Let's try again," I announce more resolutely than before. I grit my teeth and tell myself that I can do this. I've spent years believing that if I had any magical ability, it was being a weak-willed witch. I can't live the rest of my life thinking that way.

Arcturus crouches down beside the tub until he's roughly the same height as me. He brings his hand up to my face and drags my gaze to meet his. "Deep breaths," he instructs. "Don't force it. Just think about walking through the forest with the moon cascading through the trees when you come to a clearing. You're bathed in the evening light, glowing like a goddess."

I close my eyes as he speaks and try to envision the fantasy he forms with his words. Warmth fills my lungs and I let it spread across my body.

"Imagine a ball of energy in the pit of your stomach; it swallows you whole. You fall to the ground, but you're unhurt. Your vision is sharper. You can hear the critters in the forest scurrying across the ground. Your body feels powerful, more powerful than it's ever felt before. You are unbreakable."

Energy rolls through me like an electric shock lighting up all of my senses. The warmth that started in my lungs expands outward to my extremities; I feel it all over my body like the sun beating down on me in the middle of summer. And then somewhere in between hoping I can do this and thinking about how to do this, I just do it.

I'm out of the water, landing on four paws a dozen feet away. Arcturus was right. I can see as I've never seen before, my vision sharpening as I adjust to my new body. My ears prick up in detection of the sounds on a floor beneath ours. I don't feel invincible, but I feel strong. I take steps around the room as Arcturus and Fausto shout and hug one another in delight.

This is what it's like to be a shifter. To smell the

woodsy scent wafting off of Fausto while also being able to hear footsteps on a staircase outside the room. I stand on my hind legs with my paws on the window and look out over the Forbidden Lands. My human eyes could see for a few miles, but it feels like I can see for an eternity now.

Something prickles at the base of my spine and it causes me to push off the window and turn back to the room. The door to the bathroom has been flung open and Bray stands in the frame. He looks at me in shock and when I see the person standing beside him, I know that my face matches his.

"She shifted for the first time," Fausto announces proudly.

Bray shoves my father through the door and he stumbles to the ground from the force of the push. "I have her father."

If there's one thing that affects you in human form and shifted form, it's dizziness. Because the world starts spinning and I force myself to lie on the floor to keep from falling over.

Arcturus races to my side, his knees slamming into the stone as he kneels beside me. He runs his hand across my coat and whispers a few soothing words in my ear about shifting back. I must listen to him because the next time I open my eyes, I'm lying in bed and I feel like myself again.

The sound of flesh on flesh pulls me into a sitting

position. Bray's knuckles are bloody, but they're in better shape than my father's nose. "You try that shit one more time and I'll kill you, do you understand me?"

"Bray!" I gasp. "What are you doing?"

He cracks the knuckles on his unaffected hand but doesn't take his eyes off my dad. "Keeping you safe. He was going to stab you."

I don't believe it, but there *is* a knife sitting casually on the ground five feet away from them. And Arcturus is standing in front of my bed with a feral look on his face. Maybe they're onto something.

Maybe my father really *was* going to kill me.

ELSPETH

Arcturus searches through my drawers before pulling out a belt. He pulls on both ends, attempting to stretch it. "Do you mind if I use this?"

I barely shake my head no before he's on the move. Arcturus walks over to the chair that Bray has set up for my dad and orders him to place his hands behind his back.

"Elspeth," my dad begs, "call this off."

The Mad Kings turn to look at me. Even Arcturus stops fiddling with the leather belt that he's looping around my father's wrists. They're waiting for me to call them off, just like Cason is, but I only gnaw on my bottom lip and look away.

If it were my mother in the chair, I'd sing a different tune. I'm sure she's probably lied to me, too, but she's more forgiving than my father. Amaris was always more tolerant of my faults when I was younger than my dad was. Where he yelled, she gently steered me in another direction. That isn't to say that I don't love them both equally because I do. I just think my father put himself in this position and he can handle the consequences of his actions.

"Let my daughter go," my father starts to beg. "You can do whatever you want to me. Just let her go."

Arcturus snorts as he tightens the belt around Cason's wrists. "What would we possibly want with you?"

My father strains against the bonds holding him to the chair. "I'm Alize's son."

There's a knock on the bedroom door and in walks the guard from the dungeons. He carries a metal collar similar to all the other prisoners locked up below. "I was instructed to bring this to Bray," he announces to the room.

Bray strides across the room and grabs the collar, thanking the guard for his service. Then he fits it snugly around Cason's neck, ignoring the man's yells. "We can't have you shifting on us and accidentally on purpose killing your daughter."

"We don't need a Nikae male. I'm sure you know that your lineage does not pass down the crown to a male successor," Arcturus says in an informative tone. He reaches forward to flick my father's ear, causing

Cason's face to turn red with anger. "I'm curious why Alize never pushed to have a daughter though. Because you aren't an only child, right?"

He burns with anger and every ounce of it is directed at me. "I have three older brothers. After me, *Alysin* decided she was done having children. Is that enough of an explanation for you thugs?"

Out of nowhere, Cason catches a fist to the jaw. One moment Arcturus is standing behind him, the next he's jamming his knuckles straight into the side of my father's face. "Keep your attitude in check before I find a knife and turn your tongue into Swiss cheese. Do you hear me?"

Even I shiver when he makes the threat. I surreptitiously grab the blankets and pull them over the lower half of my body.

"Now, there's a high likelihood that you never leave these grounds alive. Many prisoners don't. They leave in a plastic bag and have their ashes dumped in the lake thirty miles south. But since you're Alize's son and the father of our Queen, we're going to let her decide your fate." Arcturus crouches down to explain this to my father in a condescending, know-it-all tone. "I bet if you're a good boy, she'll let you go free. But I want her to hear everything first. I want her to know all the lies you've told her. Because she deserves to make the call after she has all the facts."

Cason's eyes fall to the ground between his legs.

The Mad Kings hover around him like vultures. I silently plead with him to tell me the truth while simultaneously hoping the truth isn't that bad. After what feels like an eternity, I ask the question I've wanted to know since my parents gave up on me. "Why wasn't I ever able to shift?"

The silence in the room now collides with the growing tension. "Answer her." Bray crackles his knuckles. "We might have accidentally dislocated Elspeth's shoulder, but I'll happily dislocate yours on purpose."

The threat of violence gets Cason's mouth to work again. He mumbles something about the men being savages, but it gets lost in the commotion of the Kings yelling at him to answer me. "Alright!" He roars back. "I'm getting to it." He gives them each a personalized glare, his eyes becoming harder when he meets Bray's gaze.

"For your fifth birthday, your mother and I gave you a ring. It had been carefully crafted by the expert jewelers that create the wearables for Wearers. Except instead of enhancing your magic, it was made to suppress your abilities." Cason mumbles those last few words and it earns him my ire. "You were meant to wear it forever, but then you broke your hand at fifteen. The doctors had to cut the ring off because it was swelling like crazy."

I vaguely remember that. A nurse was in the

process of putting me under when the doctor cut the ring off. There was an immediate wave of relief that I assumed had come from relieving some of the swelling, but now that I think about it, maybe it was the magic I had inside of me finally getting a chance to stretch its fingertips. "That's when you stopped giving me lessons," I remember after a moment. "You and mom stopped trying to teach me how to shift after that."

Cason has the grace to look abashed. "We couldn't risk you finding out who you were. It didn't matter if your brothers were Nikae's kids." He glares at Arcturus. "As he said," he gestures with his chin, "Nikae males could never receive the crown. You were the only one at risk. Your brothers could pass on the genetics, but the further from Alize that it got, the more diluted the Nikae bloodline would be. So we warned them about having a girl. Any daughter traced back to them could be stolen by the shifters in the Forbidden Lands and forced to rule.

It feels like I'm at the beach. Waves crash upon the sand, filling my ears with the sound of water instead of words. I can see my father's lips moving, but I can't figure out what he's saying.

My future nieces could face the same fate that I have. The Avermo line would be tainted forever, all because my grandfather kidnapped a Queen. "Why?" I interrupt Cason. His lips clamp together in confusion. "Why did grandpa take Alize?"

Cason shrugs his shoulders the best he can with his hands tied behind his back. "I've heard a dozen different stories. Dad said it was because they were in love, because she reached out to him, because she wanted to be free of the constraints of her position." He shakes his head as he recalls all the excuses his father gave him. "I don't know if I'll ever know the truth. I just know that he told me if I had a daughter, she would forever be at risk of being kidnapped by the Kings in the Forbidden Lands. He told me to do whatever it took to keep you. And I was successful for over nineteen years."

Up until the moment the Mad Kings broke into our home and stole me from my bed in the dead of night. "Why did mom agree to this?" I don't want to hate her. I want to put her in a box of innocence and believe that she knew nothing about what my father was doing to me.

"Because she loved you from the moment she set eyes on you. She didn't want to lose you, just like I didn't. We were happy to have your brothers and we believed that if we could skate by without having a daughter, we wouldn't have to worry about the Forbidden Landers. But then she wanted one final child and it was you." He hangs his head like a whipped dog. "We couldn't risk the Kings finding out about you, so we hid you as best we could."

Anger seizes my throat, constricting my lungs with its grasping tendrils. "No, you lied to me my entire life and made me feel as if I'd let you down. You forced me to live in the shadows and learn how to brew potions and use herbs to make poultices. You made me feel unworthy to be alive." I can feel the words coming up in my throat like vomit. Wrath, fury, indignation. Years of mistreatment and being told that I wasn't enough forces them from my throat. "Put him in the dungeon. I can't look at him anymore."

With a snap of Arcturus' fingers, a guard enters the room. "Take him to Elspeth's old cell."

My father looks at me with fear and bewilderment.

"Yeah, I was imprisoned, too," I answer the unasked question. "Because even though you kept me hidden from the world, they figured out who I was. They came and took me from my home and there was nothing I could do to fight back against three wolves. This is your fault. You can stew on that while you're rotting in my former prison."

Bray straightens his spine and a smile sweeps across his face. He looks at me in a way that I've never experienced before.

"What?" I ask, feeling unsure of myself now.

The guard drags my father out of the room and I can hear him yelling as he's forced down the stairs.

Bray walks over to the end of the bed and leans up against one of the posters. "I knew you would rise to be the Queen we needed. I've always known." Arcturus and Fausto mimic his look of pride as they come closer.

For the first time in my life, I am encouraged, not disheartened. And it feels good.

FAUSTO

Arcturus is making plans to crown Elspeth within the month. From the second she was able to shift, I could see the wheels turning in his head. She might not be battle-ready just yet, but he knows that he can get her there.

Elspeth, on the other hand, is nervous. While being the Queen of the Forbidden Lands doesn't mean meeting with the people every day, shaking hands, and kissing babies, it comes with a lot of baggage.

She will have to stand before the packs and make the announcement that she's Alize Nikae's long-lost granddaughter. She'll be required to meet with the packs on their terms and get to know their needs. She'll be responsible for pulling us into a war and knowing when to retreat. There are a lot of politics that she'll have to learn from Arcturus, Bray, and me, and that's just the beginning.

Behind closed doors, she will be our wife. While there are cooks in the kitchen and guards around every corner ready and willing to facilitate all of our needs, there is only one thing that Elspeth is required to do that can't be passed on to someone else. She will have to sleep with us, all of us, and birth our children. She doesn't have to be bred like a stallion, but she needs two daughters at the least. I think the intimacy of her future scares her the most.

Elspeth is happy to take lessons from Arcturus on shifting and controlling herself while shifted. She is content to travel far and wide with Bray, meeting the smaller pockets of magical beings on the outskirts of the Forbidden Lands. She is pleased to hear about my plans to build the community into a thriving metropolis for the outcast. But when it comes to the more physical aspects of the role she's meant to play, Elspeth shies away.

"She's a virgin," Arcturus tells us again one night with frustration in his tone. He paces around the room in typical fashion, hands tight behind his back as his face is drawn into thought.

Bray kicks his feet up on the table and leans back precariously in his chair. "She can't have this her way though," he reminds the room. "She can't be the

Queen and take care of the people and run *our* world without doing her duty to the Kings."

The Queens before Elspeth knew what their role was. They might have been in charge of the Forbidden Lands, but they were in charge in the bedroom, too. They enjoyed their nightly indiscretions no matter how loud or wild they got. I guess the biggest difference is that those Queens chose their packs while Elspeth is being forced to marry and mate with the one that kidnapped her.

"What if she never comes around to being with us?" I give voice to my fears and it makes me itchy with indignation. Arcturus stops mid-stride to frown at me; I'm quick to explain myself before he can yell. "What if she takes on the mantle of being the Queen but refuses her intimate duties? What can we do? *Can* we do anything? She is a Nikae. She has the Queen's blood. Ultimately, can't *she* refuse *us* and find another pack to fulfill her needs?"

That's something that Arcturus never thought would happen. A fission of fear flits across his face before disappearing behind his mask of confidence. He pulls his shoulders back and straightens his spine, bringing himself up to his full 6'9" height. "We are not going to give her that choice. I worked too hard to take this throne. I will not lose it without a fight."

I remember when he came to power. Arcturus said

those same words in a speech to the packs. Everyone knew that to earn the crown, they'd have to take down the first point, but he said those words to instill fear in his new subjects. Arcturus Holbrook would not bow to another wolf or allow himself to be brought low by another man. If Arcturus was forced to fight for his crown, only one person was coming out alive. If it meant losing his life, so be it. He'd rather lose it all and die than be alive to watch his reputation tarnished.

"How do you propose we keep her from finding out that she doesn't have to listen to us?" We can't keep her in a prison cell forever. Besides, if she stands before the packs beaten and bruised, they'll turn on us. The moment they know that she is a Nikae, they will destroy us if they think we hurt her. We are treading dangerous waters and none of us knew that when we concocted this ridiculous plan.

Arcturus returns to pacing; he does his best thinking in motion. But it's Bray who comes up with a solution.

He snaps his fingers and draws our attention to him. "I've got it!" He announces as though a lightbulb suddenly flickered on his head. "We seduce her and take her. Now. Tonight, even."

"And if she turns us down?" I ask with a raised eyebrow.

Arcturus answers for Bray. "We don't give her that

option. If she starts protesting, we cover those protests with pleasure. We make her feel good. Then when she's too weak to resist, we fuck her into submission."

I swallow the lump forming in my throat. Something feels wrong about this, but at the same time, I know it's what we have to do. "She's supposed to be our Queen," I say weakly. "*We're* supposed to submit to *her*."

"In public," Arcturus corrects, "but behind closed doors, whatever happens, happens. If we take the Queen by force and it happens to work in our favor, so be it. She will come around, boys, because we'll make her."

A chill races down my spine. I've spent the last few years with a variety of women in the Forbidden Lands. I enjoyed the delectable taste of a witch's cunt as she sat on my face. I allowed myself in human and wolf form to ingratiate myself into a dozen different packs. I have made love and fucked some of the most beautiful women I've ever met. But none were like Elspeth.

She is young and stunning with a lithe little body that begs to be destroyed. I have dreamt about burying my face in her soft, brunette locks and breathing in her scent. It would be wrong for me to say I want to press my nose between her thighs and take a big whiff, but it's something I've wanted since the second I saw her. I've imagined doing to Elspeth every obscene and indecent thing I could think of.

What we're doing is probably wrong. If the packs knew, we might face ruination. But until the filthy, ugly truth comes out, I'm going to get my dick wet. I will have Elspeth Nikae if it kills me. And knowing how rumors travel around these parts, it just might.

ELSPETH

Another week in the Forbidden Lands. Another week in my new home.

There are too many floors and hallways for me to know the castle like the back of my hand. Sometimes I still get lost trying to find my way back to my room after an expedition in the floors above. There's always something new to find and it is my greatest joy to unearth something fresh.

The fifth-floor hallway is filled with the skulls of the previous Queens. They sit on mantels encased in glass with a small gold plate that announces their greatest victory. My great-grandmother was the last skull to be added and her contribution to the Forbidden Lands was a lasting relationship with the dragon shifters a century ago. She was a great Queen, by all accounts.

I make friends with the people who live in the castle. The kitchen staff show me how to make my favorites: roasted duck, rosemary and garlic mashed potatoes, honey-glazed carrots, and more. I introduce myself to all the guards, careful to keep my last name to myself. They don't seem very interested in me, but when I bring them sweet treats from the kitchen, they soften in my presence. I run into various members of the Council and they watch me warily. They never accept the food I've lovingly prepared or the compliments I offer like candy. They don't understand why I'm here and they make their displeasure clear.

I go everywhere and do everything, except see my father in the dungeon. I have anxiety about his presence down there. I know that the right thing to do would be to let him go, but then I'm halfway to the dungeon to release him when I'm reminded about the lies he told me all of my life. It occurs to me that I never would have lost a kidney, had my shoulder dislocated, or even had these initials branded into my skin if it wasn't for my father's untruths.

Inevitably, I will see him. I'll have to. But I am still wounded by the falsehoods he told me and it would hurt too much to see his face.

I know that my brain is playing tricks on me. The more that I blame my father, the less angry I am at the Mad Kings. And I have to be less angry with them if I'm going to survive here. I don't think they'll ever let me return home and if they did, I don't know what my place there would be like. At least here in the Forbidden Lands, I know where I stand.

I've run into the dungeon guard a few times. He moseys around to the kitchen during off-peak hours and that's often when I'm there getting lessons on how to make biscuits or cook a new dish. Only once do I speak with him, long enough to ask what happened to the guard before him. I thought about inquiring about my father, but I chicken out at the last minute. I'm afraid of what he'll tell me. So I switch to asking him about the previous guard instead.

"I don't know exactly what happened to him. He was a wizard or something and I heard a lot of rumors about his savagery. But when I was offered this position, I was told that you were a special prisoner. Don't let anyone touch you. Don't let anyone hurt you. That was the deal." He didn't have much to say, but I got the picture. The guy before him had crossed an invisible line in the sand and someone told the Kings. Wherever he was now, I doubted he was happy.

Sometimes I think about Rigo and Bilia. When the Kings hole up in the throne room and have prisoners brought to them, I'm told to leave the castle or find something to do to occupy myself. It's a reminder that they still have their rituals. They still have prisoners brought to them and they still torture them regularly.

Are my old cellmates brought to the throne room? Do they bear the bruises and blood of the Kings' hands?

Those questions always bring up a host of others. Is that something I'll have to participate in when I'm crowned Queen? Or will I be oblivious to the wrongdoings of those in the dungeons left to Kings' desires?

I hesitate when it comes to asking them hard questions like that. They're nicer now than when they kidnapped me. They're nicer now that I live on the third floor with them. I'm not afraid that they're going to turn on me and throw me back in a prison cell, but anything is possible. I've seen the way they leer at me when they think I'm not looking. I'm not afraid of going back to the prison that I came from; I'm afraid of the prison I'm about to enter.

When I was a little girl, I dreamt about my wedding day. We all do it, don't we? I looked forward to seeing all my friends and family in the audience while I stood on a platform and promised to love my husband for the rest of my life. In my dreams, he was tall and handsome with a smiling face that made my insides warm. We'd have a dozen children and live in a big home like my parents.

Marriage to the Mad Kings doesn't seem anything like that. I see the lust in their eyes when they look at me. I know that they watch me with lascivious yearning. I remember changing a few days ago when I thought no one was around. I turned to find Arcturus peering at me through the door, eyes tracing my curves as I undressed. The Mad Kings look at me as if they want to eat me alive and that terrifies me.

But if I'm being honest, in the dead of night when the moon is high and my body is restless, I remember the dinner we had together a few weeks ago. I recall Fausto's hand rubbing against me, demanding every ounce of pleasure from my body. I try to be good and just go to sleep, but some nights it's hard. My hand sneaks between my stomach and the fabric of my panties, drifting down, down, down until it finds what it's looking for. I let my fingers skate across my core the same way that Fausto's did. And when I find myself stifling my moans with a pillow so as to not wake my corridor mates, I am left unfulfilled and frustrated.

I know what they want to do to me and what marrying them means. In those moments of frustrated incompletion, I want it, too. But I'm scared. I thought that I would have love and monogamy when I finally got married, not three men waiting to sleep with me out of duty.

I wish I could talk to my grandmother. She had a pack like the Mad Kings in her youth. What was their relationship like? What can she do to prepare me for this? Will love ever come? Or will I spend the rest of my life waiting for something that doesn't exist for people like me?

ELSPETH

I'm walking through the hall of royalty when I see a flicker of light shining from inside my room. The door is cracked and the sounds of laughter and soft music flow into the hallway. *The Mad Kings,* the little voice in my head infers.

The last I saw of them, they were in the gardens. Arcturus looked upset about something and there was a lot of back and forth between the three of them, but since I was on the fifth floor of the castle, I couldn't make out what they were saying.

I knock twice before entering my own room, feeling strangely unwelcome in a space that I call my own. Arcturus is sprawled out on my bed with his hands clasped behind his head showing off his topless upper half. Fausto leans up against one of the posters of my bed with his shirt off. Bray lies on the floor and his shirt is also nowhere to be found.

"Hello," I greet tentatively as I take a few more steps into the room. "Did I miss something?" They didn't notice me come inside, but when they hear me speak, all eyes turn toward me. *Cue the self-consciousness,* I think to myself.

Bray contorts his body until he's lying on his stomach. His beautiful brown eyes travel from my toes to my nose and he licks his lips when he lingers on my chest. "Elspeth," he grins, "just the girl we were looking for."

My stomach turns over with acute anxiety. "Oh?" I struggle to maintain my confidence in the face of these three half-naked men. "And what were you looking for me for?"

Arcturus pats the spot on the bed beside him. He's taken off his shoes and rolled his pant legs up to expose his ankles; he's the epitome of casual. "Come, sit down. Chat with us."

I know that if I sit down on the bed, I'm stepping into the lion's den. Or in this case, the wolf's lair. There's no way these three men chose to wait for me in my bedroom *just* to chat about my day.

You can do this, I tell myself. *You're going to have to do it one day anyway.* I remain in my spot a few seconds longer as if glued to the floor. Though I tell my feet to move, they never seem to get the hint.

Bray pops off the floor with ease when he sees that I'm not making my way over to Arcturus. "Is something wrong, Elspeth?" He stalks toward me and I force myself to avert my eyes. His body is all hard lines and rock-hard abs. Tan skin creeps across every inch of his torso. The muscles in his biceps ripple when Bray reaches out to grab my hand and bring it to his lips. "If something's wrong, just tell us. We'll fix it for you."

He mumbles the words against the tips of my fingers and the vibration from his lips floods me with an unexpected sensation. The woman who's spent the last week touching herself beneath the blankets now screams in my ear. *This is the satisfaction you're looking for. They'll take care of your needs.* I try to shush her by telling myself I don't have any needs, but that's a comforting lie I say to make myself feel better.

"Elspeth, say something," Fausto frowns from his place against the bed.

What do I say? That I have a sinking feeling that I know what this is about? That I'm equally afraid and excited about what they're going to do to me? That this is my first time and I didn't expect it to be with all three of them *at the same time*? Instead of giving voice to my fears, I just mumble, "I think I need some water."

Fausto responds with ease. He heads for the door and snaps his fingers. In no time at all, a guard comes around the corner and asks what he needs. He makes the request before shutting the door behind him and turning to face me. "See, Elspeth? We're willing to do anything for you post-haste. What's it like to have three men waiting on you hand and foot?"

My stomach is swimming in a sea of uncertainty. The last time I had an intimate encounter with these men, I was sitting at a dinner table with Fausto's hands exploring the most private parts of me. It was the most terrifying moment of my life. And, if I'm being honest, the most erotic.

They only want to give you that again, the little voice pushes me forward. *They want to make you feel good.* It sounds contrary to the behavior they inflicted upon me just weeks before, but I believe it.

Bray swings around my body until he's standing behind me. Gently, he lets my hand fall to my side. It's only a few milliseconds later before I feel his fingers digging into the knots in my shoulders. "You're very tense. You need to relax."

Easy for him to say. He isn't torn between the fantasies of his childhood and the realities of his present situation. But I must admit, his hands are working magic. I almost forget the two men in front of me making their way across the room. I close my eyes and lean back into Bray while he massages my anxiety away.

"That's right," he whispers in my ear, "Relax, my pet. Daddy will make it all better."

His words call to the woman inside of me that craves being touched. She's the one that moans with delight as he manipulates her body with his strong hands.

I'm taken aback when my skirt raises, exposing my thighs to the coolness of the room. I try to look down, but Bray is quick. His hand leaves my shoulder to wrap around my throat, fingers pinching the sides of my neck. "No, no," Bray whispers in my ear, "don't worry about what Arc is doing. Pay attention to me." It is an order.

His other hand snakes around my waist to hold me in place. While I inhale to draw a deeper breath, my head starts to swim under the pinch of his fingers cutting off my oxygen. It is a delightful sensation that makes me squeeze my thighs in anticipation.

Arcturus hands Bray the hem of my dress. He holds the skirt aloft while slowly flexing his fingers around my throat to distract me from what's happening below. Every few seconds, I am treated to a full breath of air. Then a few seconds later, I gasp as my airways narrow.

Below my waist, I feel fingers in the waistband of my panties. The person slowly but forcefully slides the fabric down my thighs. If it wasn't for Bray's hand restraining my neck, I'd watch as Arcturus undressed the lower half of me. Instead, I have to settle for what it looks like in my head.

Dark brown eyes looking at the patch of curls across my mound. His bottom lip sucked between his teeth as he takes in the arousal glazing my opening.

I hope he's gentle. I hope it feels as good as I'm imagining in my head.

ARCTURUS

My eyes drift over Elspeth's skin in delight. I catch a smattering of stretch marks on her inner left thigh, leftover from her youth when she grew faster than her body could keep up with. My eyes graze the jagged scar that curves around her knee with thin, almost indistinguishable lines from where a doctor placed stitches. I even take in the shape of her calves, skin stretched taut across the muscle.

I have dreamt of this day since I was a boy. Perhaps all men in packs do. We imagine ourselves with a Nikae Queen. We bow before her. We lavish her with kisses. We bury our rod inside of her. It is a fantasy shaped by history and the unique beauty of the Nikae bloodline. It is a fantasy that not all men get to live out.

Bray holds Elspeth tight and I envy him for it. He has his arms wrapped around her like a vice grip and I wish that it was me. But I'm sure that he feels the same seeing me on my knees in front of her.

Fausto agreed to briefly take a step back. He got to feel Elspeth's pleasure a few weeks ago and he is more than happy to watch now. I give him a backward glance and see his hand buried in his pants. The front of the fabric is thick with his bulge and the material moves beneath his gesturing hand.

I spread Elspeth's thighs to give me better access to her center. A sparse patch of dark brown curls rests atop her mound and I bring my thumb up to run across them. They're wiry beneath my touch and the slightest bit damp. Elspeth may be a virgin, but she still has desire.

I drag my thumb away from her curls and let it brush against her clit. The soft tissue buds beneath my fingers and she makes a soft, mewling sound. She is so sensitive that it makes my dick hard.

I can't restrain myself any longer. I wanted to go slow to drive Elspeth crazy with need, to let her see what will come from loving the Kings, but I am only a man. I have a man's impulses and a man's lust and I can't keep myself from leaning forward and taking a lick.

The first dip of my tongue against her pussy is like

devouring honey straight from the hive. She is sweet like candy and I could lap her core forever.

She pulls away from me as much as she can, pushing back into Bray when she realizes what I'm doing. He tightens his fingers on the sides of her throat to keep her from arguing. It's a dirty trick and it works like a charm.

I grab her hips and hold her in place as I dive back in. I greedily lick her opening until she's gasping for air. Is it from my ministrations or Bray's choking? I don't know nor do I care; it's a sound fit for the Kings' ears only.

Elspeth pushes and pulls against all the foreign touches as if fighting with herself about what she wants. Moans slip between her lips and fill the room with the sound of her pleasure. I draw my tongue from her opening to her clit and it drives her insane. She fights for air and self-restraint, finding neither.

With my lips wrapped around her clit, I roll my tongue over the little bundle of nerves. Her thighs start to quiver around my face and I press deeper against her soft, supple skin.

If she's going to take us inside of her, she needs to be primed. I bring a thumb to her core and slowly press in. Her clit throbs as if it has its own heartbeat. Her insides are slick and warm and she only gasps for a second at the intrusion of my digit.

Once I'm sure that she can handle the girth of my

thumb, I pull it out and replace it with my index and middle fingers. Once more she sharply intakes air as I start to slowly thrust back and forth inside of her. Her cunt clamps around my fingers and I swear I'm going to come in my pants. I can just imagine what it will feel like to have her muscles gripping my cock and it makes me hard with need.

I don't make it to pushing my ring finger inside of her before she's orgasming around me. She grinds her pussy against my mouth and hand as she takes her pleasure. Her body feels like it's twenty degrees hotter as she rides my face, a thin layer of sweat forming around her navel.

Behind me, the sound of Fausto coming in his pants almost tears me away from Elspeth's pleasure. He groans loudly as he creams all over the cloth, swearing only moments later when he realizes what he's done. It's a frustrating distraction from the gorgeous woman writhing around me.

"Hot," she whispers, enough of a word to get Bray to loosen his grip on her throat. "I-I'm hot."

Fausto, stripping down to nothing at all, offers to take care of that for her. "Let me get you out of this dress." He nearly steps on me as he approaches, kicking my leg instead in an unspoken demand for me to get out of the way.

I carefully withdraw from Elspeth's center and sit back on my haunches. She looks down at me uneasily and I give her a wink before popping my wet digits in my mouth. A blush colors her cheeks as she watches me suck her juices off my fingers. "Delicious," I grin when I finish.

Bray twists her in his grip until she's facing him again. "Hello, gorgeous," he says as he looks down at her.

From behind, Fausto fiddles with the zipper on her dress. As he exposes her flawless, naked back, I have to readjust myself. It's been a while since I was last with a woman; that's probably why seeing her disrobed back has me rock hard.

"Tonight, you're ours," Bray whispers to Elspeth. "Tonight you will find out the pleasure of being with a pack."

She must falter. Even as Fausto manipulates her body to pull the dress down, Elspeth hesitates in Bray's arms. "I don't know if I'm ready for that," she whispers in a low, hesitant tone.

In a move that devastates me to the core, Bray leans down to press his lips to hers. I might have been the first person to go down on Elspeth, but he takes her first kiss. I love my pack mate, but I can't deny the jealousy bubbling in my bloodstream.

"You're ready," Bray tells Elspeth without a hint of doubt in his tone. "Now let's get you on the bed so we can prove it."

ELSPETH

Am I the only one trembling like a schoolgirl on her first day of classes? As Bray leads me to the bed, my legs feel like concrete with every step that I take. My thighs are still shaking from Arcturus' wicked tongue. Or maybe it's from fear of what's coming next.

"Let me get on the bed first," Bray whispers as he presses a hand to my shoulder. "I want to feel you on top of me." He starts to disrobe and my eyes fall to his member. A forest of hair sprouts in every direction, all leading back to his cock. I could wrap both of my hands around it and still not touch the base and tip at the same time.

A few minutes ago, Arcturus' fingers felt like they were opening me up. They stretched the tissue inside my vagina and even through the shock of pain from the size, it felt good. But that was only two fingers. "I can't take that," I insist, meeting Bray's eyes so he knows that I'm serious. When he doesn't respond, I turn to Arcturus and Fausto to plead with them for help.

They are no help.

Fausto might have just masturbated while watching Arcturus go down on me, but his cock is already weeping with renewed desire. He's a few centimeters shorter than Bray, but his girth makes my stomach churn.

And everything about Arcturus is large from the span of his hands to the size of his member. He's hung like a God damn horse and I know that if I can't take Bray inside of me, there's no way I'm getting all of Arcturus in.

"Wait a second," I start to take a step back but Bray grabs me by the wrist to stop me. "I can't do this. Those-those *things*," I avoid eye contact with them, "aren't going to fit. I'm not-I can't." The words keep coming out of my mouth like vomit. My heart is pounding and my fight-or-flight response is screaming at me to run away.

But the Mad Kings are nicer than they appear. Bray's grip on my wrist loosens and he grabs his cock instead. He meets my gaze and says, "This isn't going to hurt you. It's soft flesh that, even hard, is no match for a fist or club. It isn't going to plow through you or damage anything. Your body will take it just fine because that's what bodies are meant to do. You'll even like it because it feels good."

Arcturus nods his head in agreement. "We mean you no harm, Elspeth. You might be a Queen of the blood, but you mean more to us than that. You're going to be our wife and the mother of our children. You are the only woman we'll look at from now until the day we die. We don't want to taint that relationship by hurting you."

My nerves start to lessen but not without leaving newly formed knots in my shoulders. "Can-can I ask a question first?" They all nod their heads at varying speeds. "I know it's silly of me, but I thought that when I got married, it would be for love. I know I can't go back to the Cersei district or even probably Meira'mor at all, but a part of me still hopes that love will come one day."

Anxiety wells up in my chest again and I try to quiet it with a tap of my fingers against my thigh. *This is your life now, Elspeth. You have to embrace it.* The little voice in my head is right. Whatever happens next, I have to live and die by the choices my family has made for the last sixty years. "Will we ever love one another?" My voice breaks and I want to kick myself for sounding so weak.

"Yes," Fausto takes a step forward. "I think in a twisted, sick kind of way, *we* love *you*. We wouldn't have risked our lives to steal you from the mainland if we didn't." He looks at the floor and the room stays silent for a few pressing moments as Fausto gathers his thoughts. "We don't know what you like to do in your spare time or what your feelings are on all of this. We haven't been as attentive to your needs as we should have been. But I promise you that that changes today."

Arcturus opens his mouth to speak, but Fausto pierces him with a look. The first point of the crown slowly brings his lips back together, giving Fausto the floor once more. "If anyone has to worry, it's us. You can give us up, Elspeth. You can decide that we aren't the ones for you. Our rule only exists as long as we're by your side."

Fausto takes a few more steps closer until he's only an arm's length away, then he reaches out to grab my hand. "I know that we have no right to ask you to stay with us after all that we did. We kidnapped you and imprisoned you in less-than-optimal conditions. We injured you time and time again. We lashed out at you when you didn't follow our instructions or simply had a different opinion. That's our fault and all we can do is apologize for our behavior. But please, Elspeth, know that none of that will ever happen again." He squeezes my hand as if to reassure me that his words are true. "We are yours now, for as long as you'll have us."

I've always wanted a grand romantic gesture. I wanted my boyfriend to chase me through the streets in the pouring rain just so that he could kiss me for the very first time. I wanted my fiancé to plan an elaborate proposal that I'd remember for the rest of my life. I wanted my husband to build me a home as a love letter to the way he felt about me.

But those were dreams and this is reality. Fausto isn't chasing me through the streets. Bray isn't on his knee proposing. And Arcturus isn't building me a home.

"Okay," I decide. I pull my hand out of Fausto's but not out of malice. I give myself room to look around at the three men before me. We all stand here naked, our truest selves, something that I've never experienced before. These three men have been honest with me from the start, even when it hurt. I can cut them a little slack considering all they've done for me. "I'll try. I'll give it my best shot." I still don't think that ramrod of a cock on Arcturus is going to fit inside of me, but I'll let him do his best.

Morning comes too quickly. The first light to shine through the windows wakes me up. Sprawled out around me are the Kings, all in various stages of repose. I extract myself from their web of arms and legs and make my way to the bathroom.

Every part of me is sore, even body parts that I don't remember using last night. I draw a bath and fill the water with sweet-smelling floral scents and salts. I open the curtains and let natural light into the bathroom, bathing every surface in gold. Then I sink to my chin in the tub and let the hot water soothe my aching body.

Last night was almost more than I could bear. It was the semblance of love I didn't know that I needed.

Bray was the first to enter me. He laid on the bed and helped position me above his cock. I could see his veins straining under my weight as he held me aloft and slowly lowered me onto him. Fausto joined from behind, reducing some of the load his friend had to carry.

It was the perfect cock to impale me for the first time. He wasn't as long as Arcturus or as thick as Fausto. He was a flawless blend of the two of them, opening me up and tenderly getting me used to the feeling of someone inside of me.

The first time I saw Bray, I wanted to get as far away from him as possible. But last night I let him touch me in ways that no other man had. Despite his former brackish behavior, he was sweet and gentle with me. He didn't even mind the few droplets of blood that coated his cock as he thrust inside me for the first time.

Fausto knelt behind me through the whole thing. While Bray held my hips in place, Fausto played with my breasts. His fingers tweaked and pulled my nipples until they were hard little pebbles in his hands. He placed a mark on my neck with his teeth, dragging them over my tender skin until it started to change colors.

He took me when Bray and I had finished. He didn't seem to mind that my pussy was full of another man's come. He laid me down beside Bray and entered me gently from above. "Are you alright?" He asked as his thick member stretched me again.

I nodded my head and let him guide me. Bray helped me lift my leg over Fausto's hip and showered me in kisses when the pleasure of the cock inside me took me over the edge. I could have fallen asleep right then, but Arcturus had waited patiently at the end of the bed. He watched as the two men in his pack deflowered me. When it was finally his turn, he crawled in between Bray and me and had me roll over onto my side.

I could feel his cock pressing against my ass as he slowly rolled his hips back and forth. He draped an arm over my waist and let his tongue tickle the skin that Fausto had previously sucked on. "You are ours, Elspeth." He entered me from behind, still in our intimate embrace. "Every breath you take belongs to us now." He thrust forward and back until I could feel the base of his cock disappearing inside of me. The other two men had prepared me for his entrance and I gobbled him whole. "Every need you have is ours to fulfill." Arcturus lasted the longest. He fucked me the hardest. "Every desire you have is ours to satisfy." And when I came, it was with an unearthly scream. "We took you and you are ours forever."

I ache today, that's true. My body hurts in all the reasonable places: my pussy, my thighs, my ass. But I hurt in other places, too. My calves are sore from stretching my legs out in pleasure when I was racked with an orgasm. My toes hurt from curling into the bedsheets every time someone's cock hit me just right. My arms feel like they got a workout from gripping the blankets to keep from shattering into a thousand pieces.

The bath will help. The salts will ease my aches and pains. And then later, we can renew them in other places and positions.

It turns out that love isn't just black or white. It can be the shades of gray in between. Love is found in the little things. Like Arcturus waiting for his pack mates to enjoy me first, putting aside his needs for the good of our newly formed union. Or the way Fausto distracted me from the brief frisson of pain that I felt when Bray first entered me. Or how the three of them promised to stay all night because they wanted to make sure that I was okay physically *and* mentally.

Love will come, I have no doubt about that. The Mad Kings have done terrible, unforgivable things in the past. But they're just the Kings to me now.

My Kings.

ELSPETH

One of the hardest truths you have to
face in life is yourself.

I wake in the middle of the night feeling restless
and at first, I can't figure out why. It isn't
because the Kings are missing, though their
absence from my bed is notable. When I fell asleep
three hours ago, they were loitering in my room with
brown liquor. It's amazing that I fell asleep in the first
place considering they were sitting around my fireplace telling crude jokes. But that isn't weighing
on me.

I get up and grab a glass of water from the bathroom. I take it back to the sitting area in front of the

fireplace and sip it while trying to figure out what's keeping me up.

It's been two days since I surrendered my virginity to the Kings. Fausto kept his promise that they wouldn't keep anything from me anymore. I've learned more about the Forbidden Lands and the packs that I'm about to rule over than I ever cared to know. Arcturus informed me of a possible rebellion and who we would need to target within that alliance to break it up. Fausto knew the intimate details of their relationships and Bray had detailed plans of how the Kings were going to infiltrate the alliance and kill the leader. All in all, it's been an incredibly informative forty-eight hours.

But that isn't it. I have too much information floating around my head between the politics of leadership and the role I'm supposed to play, but what plagues me is deeper than that.

The answer hits me like a brick wall. Three stories beneath my feet is the man keeping me awake. Now that my conscience has been unburdened of the future between the Kings and myself, it is free to think about more important things. Like the man I have rotting in the basement because I can't stand to look at his face.

You should let him go, the little voice in my head announces gleefully. *Then he can't bother you anymore.* But I have a sinking feeling that it isn't that simple.

There will always be unanswered questions that only my father knows the answer to.

Perhaps that's what leads my feet. It isn't the weight on my shoulders or the worry that my father will die in the dungeon; it's the questions I want to ask before I never have the chance to do so again.

I grab a robe on my way out of the door and wrap the soft, velvety material around my body like a second skin. It protects me against the draft in the hallways as I make my way through the maze of doors and stairwells until I find myself lingering a few feet away from my father's prison.

They put him in my old cell, just like they said they would, but the guard took away all of the extra blankets Roth had gotten me that first night. My father lays still on the concrete cot with a single woolly strip of cloth draped over the upper half of his body.

"Father," I call to him but he doesn't stir. "Dad," I raise my voice a little louder and this punctures the blanket of sleep. "Cason!" I demand in a sharper tone and this, finally, wakes him from his rest.

Cason lifts his head from the bed with a bewildered look on his face. It takes him a few seconds to adjust his eyes and get a bead on me, but when he does, a smile breaks out over his face as he scrambles to sit upright. "Elspeth, you're alive!" He breathes in delight.

"Of course, I'm alive," I frown. "Why wouldn't I be?"

He gets up from the cot and makes his way toward the bars. My father wisely doesn't reach out for me but instead wraps his fingers around the bars of the cage he's in. "The Mad Kings," he says as if that's all the explanation I need.

I don't call them that anymore. Not in my thoughts and not aloud. Arcturus, Fausto, and Bray have done some terrible things, but it was all in the name of protecting the Forbidden Lands and its residents. "I am to be their Queen, dad. They wouldn't hurt me." As long as you don't count the time Fausto dislocated my shoulder. Or when they kept me in a prison cell after I had a kidney removed and everything hurt. Or even that time they carved their initials into my shoulder with a blade. But besides that, they wouldn't hurt me.

Cason doesn't look like he believes me. He shrugs his shoulders and stays pressed against the bars. "Are you here to let me go?" He asks, quickly changing the subject.

The voice in my head urges me to say yes, but I can't convince my lips to form that response. "What happens if I do?" I stall for time instead, waiting for him to say the right thing. Anything that will get the weight of his existence down here off my shoulders. His presence gnaws at me like a rat at cheese and I want it to go away.

My father's grip on the bars loosens just a bit. I see blood rush back into his white knuckles and watch as the skin turns a shade pinker. "I-I go back home," he stammers. "Then I will do my best to save you, Elspeth."

During my childhood, he read me a thousand bedtime stories where the damsel in distress was saved by the handsome prince on a white horse. When the stories ended, I asked to hear them again and again because I wanted to be the damsel in distress that needed to be saved. But that was when I was a child. I've grown since then. I've been exposed to the real world. "Don't," I whisper.

Cason's grip slackens even more as his hands fall down the bars until they rest at his side. "Don't what?" He questions with a frown deepening on his face.

I take a deep breath and swallow down the bile that threatens to fill my throat. A few weeks ago, I was kidnapped in the dead of night by three men that I only knew as the Mad Kings. I was under the impression that they meant to rape, torture, and kill me, but that was all due to my father's teachings. Crazily enough, that's not what they wanted, not really. And it's that realization that spurs me forward.

"I don't need to be saved. I am not a damsel in distress. I am a Queen and I am exactly where I'm supposed to be." I believe what I say and that's the most important piece of the puzzle. My father has been down here biding his time until he dies or sees the light of day again. I've let him wither away hoping that he would be the key to my freedom if I needed it. But I don't need the answers he has anymore, they'll only make me more angry. And I don't need him to protect me anymore. I don't need him.

Cason scrambles to agree with me. He adamantly nods his head yes and raises his hands in surrender. "Of course, you don't, honey. You're stronger than I thought you were. You can get yourself home."

I close my eyes to drown him out of my sight. "*This* is my home now, dad. Don't you understand that?" When I open my eyes, he's taken a few steps back and wears a look of confusion on his face. "I'm not coming back to Meira'mor proper. I'm staying here in the Forbidden Lands. Forever."

His spirit looks crushed and I take an ounce of joy from it. After all, he nearly ruined my life. "Elspeth," he buries his face in his hands, "what am I supposed to tell your mother?"

Both of them have been lying to me since I was old enough to understand them. They were in it together to keep my shifter abilities suppressed. God knows who else in the Cersei district got involved in their little scheme to hide the Nikae from the wolves in the outcast district. "Tell her the truth. Tell her I'm dead. Tell her whatever helps you sleep at night. It isn't my problem anymore. *You* aren't my problem anymore."

I turn my back on my father and start to walk away. A few seconds later, I hear him slam his body against the cell doors. "Elspeth," he begs, "please, let me out. Come home with me. Things will change. You're a shifter now. I can teach you to harness your abilities and use them for good."

I want to tell Cason that I've been a shifter all along no thanks to him. I want to yell that I wouldn't give up my queenly duties to be his daughter again even if it came with a fortune, a crown, and the happily ever after I dreamt about as a child. But instead, I just keep walking.

I came down here to have all of my lingering questions answered. But the truth is, I don't need him to answer anything for me. A deep exploration into why he forced this life upon me isn't going to make me feel better. Understanding why my grandfather kidnapped Alize sixty years ago won't make me a stronger person. Knowing the past isn't relevant anymore.

I am the Queen of the Forbidden Lands and I won't let anyone take that away from me.

FAUSTO

We thought about crawling into bed with Elspeth when we finished drinking, but she looked so peaceful. With dark locks splayed across the pillow and her eyes shut in respite, we couldn't bring ourselves to interrupt her sleep.

Instead, we left her room and parted ways. Arcturus headed to the roof. I know because he always seems to get introspective when he drinks. He carried the bottle of bourbon with him and headed to contemplate the future under the midnight moon. Bray mentioned eating, then switched his words to archery. I couldn't imagine shooting a bow in the dark while drunk was a good idea, but I wasn't going to stop him.

I settled into my room with a journal and a glass of water to stave off tomorrow's impending hangover. In the pages scored with pen marks were ideas for the Forbidden Lands, like the currency I once wanted to create and a plan for harvesting lumber from the mainland districts without getting caught. My journal is a silly little book full of policies and procedures that I may never get around to implementing. Arcturus suggested that I write them down so I could see them on paper and think out implementation and application.

I flip to a blank page and start sketching out the Queen's rooms. We need a bigger bed and probably another couch in front of the fire. This way we can spend more time with Elspeth without feeling cramped. We don't have to do all of our planning in the throne room or around a great table. We can plan while draped in silks and smelling of sex. When she gets pregnant, it'll be easier for her to rise from bed and walk to the sitting area than it will be for her to make it down a couple of flights of stairs to the dining room. I want her bedroom to be comfortable and versatile for all of our needs.

I spend almost an hour drawing out plans and writing ideas in half-distinguishable chicken scratch before a knock on the door stops me in my tracks. I tap the pen in frustration against the paper before suppressing my irritation. "It's open."

I expect a guard or Bray. I expect Arcturus to come and ask me about some crazy idea he had on the roof of the castle. But I get Elspeth instead. She's wrapped in a silk black robe and looks dwarfed in comparison to the large opening of the door. "Hey," I greet her with a smile. "You okay? It's a little late to be wandering the halls." I have a fleeting thought that she might be trying to escape, but it disappears in the next second. If Elspeth wanted to leave, she could easily make her way out of the castle without stopping by my room first.

"I need you to take my father home." It isn't a question or a plea, it's a command.

I set my journal to the side and get out of my chair. "Elspeth, what's going on?"

She takes a few more steps into the room and a beam of moonlight catches her face; she looks resolute. "I want you to take him back to the Cersei district. Now. Release him and promise me that you'll never set your sights on him again."

That wasn't something I'd planned to do tonight. "I'll need to talk to Arcturus and Bray first, but I think-"

Elspeth cuts me off with a single hand held up to stop me. "No. I need you to do it right now. I need him gone."

I'm tempted to turn her down and send her back to her room, but that isn't what a King would do for his Queen. Something is bothering Elspeth and it's my responsibility to take care of it. "Of course. I'll take care of it first thing in the morning."

She crosses the space between us until she's only a few inches away from me. Elspeth reaches up to place a hand on my chest and it draws out the inner protector in me. She is so small in comparison; she is so delicate. "Now, Fausto. I won't be able to sleep until he's gone."

She doesn't have to say anything else. I don't know what her motives are, but I don't care. Elspeth looks bereft to even have to speak these words. And I would move heaven and Earth for my Queen. "I'll do it now. I promise." I cover her hand with mine and feel the warmth of her skin on mine. She gives me a half-smile and mouthes '*thank you*'.

"I'll be back in a few hours. Do you want me to come to see you when I get back?" Elspeth nods her head yes and seems unable to form words. That's okay. She doesn't have to speak. "I'll see you soon." I lean down to press my lips to hers before tearing myself away from her. The place where her hand used to lie on my chest feels cold in the absence of her touch.

I consider what I'm going to tell Arcturus and Bray as I head down the stairs. Would they do this if she asked? What would their reasoning be?

There is a row of keys hanging in the dungeon affixed to the wall. Since the guard is likely asleep in his quarters, I grab the key to Cason's cell and make my way down to him. I see that he's awake, his back pressed against the wall as he stares at the ceiling. Did Elspeth tell him what she was going to do? Once more, I second-guess her intentions.

Cason feels my presence because, after a moment, he turns his head to look at me. "She sent you to let me go," he deduces quickly.

I slip the key into the lock and twist it until the mechanism opens. "Elspeth doesn't want you in the castle anymore." I'm burning inside with curiosity. What happened? What did I miss in the couple of hours since we left Elspeth's room?

"What did you say to her?" He asks as he slowly gets to his feet. "Why does she want to stay?"

My heart soars to hear him say that. I thought that Elspeth would eventually get around to feeling like this was her home, but I hadn't realized that it'd happen so soon. "We loved her, is all," I tell him with a shrug. It would be hard to explain what happened. Bray would take great joy in telling Elspeth's father that we deflowered his daughter and that's what changed her mind, but I'm a kinder soul. Or at least I am today.

Cason walks through the door and looks up at me. He is only a couple of inches shorter, but I have more muscle and bulk and strike a more imposing figure. "*I* loved her."

Maybe that's true; she *is* his daughter after all. But

his love turned her into a frightened, scared little girl that looked around every corner for the boogeyman to pop out and snatch her. Our love set her free from that fear. "Maybe that's the problem."

He squares off his shoulders and straightens his back like he might reach forward with a fist. But either he knows better or he realizes that it'd be asking for trouble because Cason eventually huffs at me instead. "I don't know what you said to my daughter, but I'm going to make you regret it. She should be at home with me, not pandering to your outdated notions of royal blood and sovereignty. The fact that the Meira'mor government allows *you people* to exist is beyond me."

Elspeth told me to remove him from the castle and take him back to the Cersei district. She *didn't* say that I needed to do it without giving him a black eye. I pop my elbow forward and let it collide with his cheekbone. The sound of bone cracking is followed by a roar of pain. "Nobody *allows* us to exist, so you can just get that out of your head right now. We exist, period. And if you ever step foot in the Forbidden Lands again, I'll kill you and bury the body before Elspeth even has a chance to find out that you were here. Are we clear?"

Cason is gripping his face with one hand and snarling at me. The collar around his neck is the only thing protecting me from him shifting and trying to rip out my throat. "You'll let my daughter go. I won't rest until she's free."

I could hit him again, but what's the use? It's clear that Cason has a one-track mind and nothing I say is going to change that. "She'll be our wife soon, just remember *that*. And we'll fight twice as hard to keep her as you will to steal her back."

If he has any other witty quips or threats he wants to utter, he can say them to himself. I grab his arm and drag him behind me as I make my way upstairs. Elspeth wanted him gone and that's what I'm going to do. I don't care what kind of war this starts. Cason Avermo will never see his daughter again as long as I'm alive.

ELSPETH

I stand before the full-length mirror and admire the royal gown chosen for my coronation. The Kings said that all the Queens before me wore something similar, the only difference being the slight updates in style and trends as the decades passed. I feel like a Queen in this deep velvet red.

Two months ago I was awakened in the dead of night to the sound of screams and yelling. My heart jumped into my throat as I scrambled to my closet door. If I would have made it, I would have found a hidden entrance that put me in the walls of the mansion. They would have taken me down, down, down until I was beneath the ground. I would have escaped.

But my fingers barely touched the doorknob when I was grabbed around the waist and hoisted backward by a wolf I'd never met before. Larger than all of my family members with devilishly red eyes, the wolf leaped from my bedroom window to the ground with me in his grasp and it was the start of my new life.

No one would envy my first few weeks in the Forbidden Lands. No one wants to be tossed in a dingy, dirty cell and left to rot while the men upstairs conspired to put you on a throne you'd never heard of before. That's the kind of thing that happens to someone else and when you read about it in the newspaper, a shiver runs down your spine and you thank God that you're okay.

But when it happens to you, everything changes.

I've never lived on such a bland diet. I think they served me venison once. There was no flavor to the meat, just a gamey texture that made my stomach turn as I ate it. But protein was a rarity in the dungeons and I had to get my fill no matter what.

My friend group shrunk to two very strange individuals. Rigo, who'd started a conspiracy to dethrone the Kings and wound up in prison because of it. And Bilia, who'd slept with Bray and then tried to murder him while he rested afterward. I didn't blame them at the time because being stolen from the only home you've ever known and being caged like an animal can make you hate anyone.

Rigo and Bilia are still down there and I think about them often. I've asked the Kings to pardon them for their crimes, but they're hesitant to do so. While Rigo seems like he's converted given my royal status, Bilia still snarls at them when she's brought upstairs for questioning and another round of torture. I don't participate in those sessions.

I could stomach a few minutes once. I remember the gaunt face of a young woman that looked barely out of her teen years. I could count her ribs through the thin, disgusting shirt that she wore. They told me that she'd killed an entire pack's pups while they were playing at the schoolyard. I wanted to see her get what she deserved, but I wasn't too keen on the sight of blood. When her lip burst open, I left the room.

I don't want to be the Mad Queen. I know that while I don't think of Arcturus, Fausto, and Bray as the Mad Kings anymore, the mainlanders still do. All they know is the death and destruction that these three men foisted upon the Cersei district since their rule began. I'm afraid that they'll think I'm just like them.

I've spent the days leading up to my coronation doodling in a journal that Fausto gave me. He said that it would help me get my thoughts and feelings down on paper. The first few pages are filled with the ramblings of a scared young woman trying to decide what kind of Queen she wants to be. I'm not sure I really understand what it means to be a Queen, but I'm learning every day.

I also spend a little bit of every day in my wolf

form. Sometimes it's with the Kings because they say it's faster to patrol the perimeter of the Forbidden Lands when we're running together. On other days it's by myself as I get a feel for my body.

I can only admit in the pages of my journal that my new form feels foreign to me. It's like trying to get to know a stranger. But every day feels like progress. Every day feels like a step in the right direction.

The scars left by the AFB initials carved into my shoulder are visible in the mirror. The cut of the dress does not hide the fact that I've been branded. But I draw my fingers over the silvery lines and feel my heart swell with excitement.

The day they chiseled these into my skin, I was brutally attacked by my father's men. I thought they'd come to save me, but the truth was darker than that. Their mission was to save or destroy the goods. Garth is somewhere in the dungeons of the castle because he was caught during the raid, but I can't bear to speak to him again. I might have released my father, but I don't have the same love for a member of his pack. Garth was like an uncle to me, but now he's nothing.

If I'm honest with myself, I've been through the wringer these past eight weeks. The Kings tell me that everything will settle down after my coronation and our wedding. I don't know what I'll do when life is back to normal. But frankly, I don't know what normal is going to look like.

"Elspeth." Arcturus knocks on my cracked door as he walks in, calling my name first so as to not startle me. "I wanted to come and see if you needed any help."

I catch his figure in the mirror and smile when our eyes meet. He is quite handsome today with his hair neatly combed and his clothes fitted well. Black is definitely his color. With his large, impressively cut frame, he grabs the attention of whatever room he's in. "No, I think I'm okay."

Arcturus walks over nonetheless. He picks off a few pieces of lint from the back of my dress before smoothing out the remaining wrinkles, then he meets my gaze in the mirror and cocks his head. "You're going to be a great Queen. You know that, right?"

I wonder if he can hear my heart thumping as loudly as I can. It sounds like a drum beating endlessly in my ears. "I guess." I wish my voice sounded more confident, but I can't bring myself to be something that I'm not.

He places his hands on the curve of my hips and holds me comfortingly in his grasp. "I'd known forever that I was going to be the King one day. I mean, look at me," he grins, "I'm huge. I knew as a teenager that I had to start preparing to take over. I had all those years to learn what it meant to be a good leader and I still made some bad decisions when I came to power.

It happens to the best of us. No one person's rule is ever perfect."

Tell that to the Queens on the fifth floor. They may only be skeletal remains, but I swear they judge me every time I walk by them. I draw my fingers across the gold plates with the commendations and I wonder if historians will ever have something good to say about me. "I know that this is my destiny," I struggle to get the words out just how I want them, "but how do I know that I'll be any good at this?"

Arcturus pulls me into him and I let the warmth of his body blanket my fears. "You don't, Elspeth, that's my point. I knew that I would be the first point of the crown one day, that I would be King alongside my pack, but I was just as nervous as you on the day I was coronated. I'd won the crown fair and square from the pack before me, and yet I had all these same fears."

I wonder if Alize felt this way the day that she was sworn into power. "What did you do to stop them from making you nervous?"

"Honestly?" Arcturus asks. I nod my head yes. "I drank a couple of glasses of ale before I went outside. That calmed my nerves. Then Bray and Fausto stood by my side and told me that if anyone dared to laugh at anything I said, they'd rip them to shreds. It was just the motivational speech I needed."

That was very kind of his pack, but it isn't what I need. "I don't know if that helped," I tell him quietly.

He nods his head slowly as if he understands. "I know. Your rule is different than the Queens before you. It's different than the Kings that had ruled in your grandmother's absence. This isn't an outcome that was ever prepared for because how were we supposed to expect it?"

Arcturus leans down to drop a kiss on my head. It's gentle and sweet and fills me with a renewed sense of peace. "But I think this means you'll have a chance to create your own rule. You can be as soft and gentle as you'd like, or you can start a war with the mainlanders this afternoon. You can do whatever you want, Elspeth. You are a Nikae. No one will dare to defy you."

I don't want to start a war with the mainlanders, at least not today. As long as my father leaves me alone, I'm happy to never return to the Cersei district. "I'll find a happy middle," I decide with a hesitant smile. "One where everybody doesn't hate me but they still fear me a little bit."

His grip on me tightens. "Whatever you want, Bray, Fausto, and I will back you up."

It turns out that all I need to give me a little courage is the strength of my men.

I wiggle out of Arcturus' grip and re-straighten the bits of fabric that wrinkled while he was holding me. "Okay. I'm ready." I decide. As ready as I'll ever be, anyway. "Crown me Queen."

HAVE YOU LEFT A REVIEW?

Reviews help new readers determine if a book is right for them. I would appreciate it if you left a review or recommended Stolen Queen on Bookbub.